FLAVOR OF THE DAY

MELLANIE SZERETO

Enjoy!
Mellanie Szereto

amatoria press

Flavor of the Day
Copyright © 2019 Mellanie Szereto
Published by Amatoria Press

ISBN-13: 978-1-942522-18-8
ISBN-10: 1942522185

Cover art by Dragonfly Press Design
Cover art and logos Copyright © 2019 Dragonfly Press Design

All rights reserved.

No part of this book may be reproduced in any form or by any electronic or mechanical means, including information storage and retrieval systems, without written permission from the author. To request permission to excerpt portions of this book, except in the case of brief quotations for reviews, please contact the author at mellanieszereto@hotmail.com.

This story is a work of fiction, and any resemblance to real persons and/or events is coincidental.

BOOKS BY MELLANIE SZERETO

Love on the Menu series ~

Love Served Hot

Red Hot Pepper

Love on the Menu...Extra Hot standalones ~

Just Desserts

Iced Latté

A Little Appetizer

The Main Dish

Dressing on the Side

Flavor of the Day

Love on the Menu…Steamed trilogy ~

Egging Her On

Sweetening Her Up

Reeling Her In

Love on the Menu: Steamed Boxed Set

Death Benefits ~ A short paranormal romance

The Sextet Anthologies ~

Volume 1: Sharing

Volume 2: Dirty Dancing

Volume 3: Occupational Hazards

Volume 4: Entanglements

Volume 5: Mistletoe & Ménage

The Sextet Presents standalones ~

Playing in the Raine: A Toy Story

Bound by Voodoo: Legends

Bewitching Desires series ~

Two if by Sea

Two Knights of Passion

Two Fated for One

Two Pirates to Treasure

Two Times the Trouble

Two Roped and Ready

Two from the Triangle

Beyond Bewitching

Writing Tip Wednesday series ~

Writing Tip Wednesday: The Writing Craft Handbook

Writing Tip Wednesday: The Writing Career Handbook

Writing Tip Wednesday: The Self-Publishing Handbook

Writing Tip Wednesday: Books 1-3 Boxed Set

CHAPTER 1

Roma Denata tapped her booted toe against the pavement and re-crossed her bare arms under her breasts. A slight chill seeped through the cinder blocks of Monte's Auto Service, but it was nothing compared to the ice in her veins.

The dark garage stall to her left stood as empty as her mechanic's skull. If he wasn't a damn magician with her Barracuda's 383 big-block, she wouldn't hesitate to make him her ex-mechanic and tell him to take the begging-for-a-date stuff and shove it up his ass. Sex and business weren't compatible, especially when sex was, more often than not, a one-off in her world.

Dating? A grave-walking shiver skittered up her spine.

The familiar roar of her baby's engine from the street soothed the creepy crawlies until she caught sight of the driver—a fuchsia-haired wench who looked to be barely old enough to have a license. Cliff sat in the passenger seat with a shit-eating grin on his stupid mug. Then his eyes locked on Roma's. Even from twenty feet away, his mouthed "oh shit" was unmistakable.

She stepped out of the shadows and into the rising heat of the early-morning sun as the car screeched to a stop a hairsbreadth from the garage door. The motor choked and rattled as Barry stalled and rolled backward several inches. Her temper flared hotter when Cliff's little playmate flicked a smoldering cigarette butt out of the window.

I don't give a damn if I have to spend the next decade searching for a new mechanic. That dickhead is never touching this masterpiece again. "Get your asses out of my car."

The girl rolled her eyes and then engaged her joyride partner in a sloppy kiss, making Roma wish she'd forgone her breakfast of last night's leftover pancetta pasta and cannoli.

She yanked open the driver's door and pulled the keys from the ignition. "Get the fuck out. Now."

Cliff scrambled away from his jailbait girlfriend and out of the passenger side. "I can explain, honey."

"Don't call me honey, you piece of shit. You let somebody drive my car without my permission. I'm reporting you to Monte when he gets back from vacation. You'll be lucky if you have a job after this stunt." Giving the girl a warning glare, Roma rounded the tight backend of the 'Cuda. A surge of satisfaction soothed her anger when Cliff backed away from her. "I told you I don't tolerate bullshit, especially where my car's concerned. We're done."

"But…" His gaze flicked toward the youngster climbing out of the driver's seat. "I was drunk, and she was flirting with me. I didn't ask for a lap dance."

The girl's chin dropped. "You grabbed my boob and—"

"Go home, little girl, before your mommy and daddy call the police to report you missing." Roma clenched her fist, making the keys dig into her palm. "And I don't give a flying fuck who you sleep with, Cliff. It's not like I ever will."

Her ex-mechanic's cheeks flushed almost as crimson as his redneck DNA. "Come on, Roma. I made a mistake. Can't you give a guy a second chance?"

"*Và al diavolo.*"

A horrified sob came from the opposite side of the car. "A mistake?"

Not even glancing toward his caterwauling plaything, Cliff

scrunched up his reddened face. "What the hell does diablo sauce have to do with anything?"

Roma turned her back on the fool and stomped to the front end of her car to check for scratches and dings. "*Diavolo*, not diablo, you moron. It's a little Italian saying my *nonna* taught me."

"So what's it mean?"

"Go to hell." Not seeing any visible signs of damage, she moved to the rear bumper.

"That's rude, even for you. Why won't you just tell me?"

"Jesus, no tune-up is worth putting up with a guy who's dumber than a stump. It means go to hell, although the literal translation is go to the devil." Not bothering to hide a chuckle at the pouty girl's huffy march along the sidewalk away from the garage, Roma finished her assessment of the driver's side. "As in, go burn in the fiery blazes of eternal damnation, you shithead. You're damn lucky you and the teeny-bopper didn't scuff the paint job, or I'd string you up from the hydraulic lift…by your balls."

Not waiting for a response, she slid behind the steering wheel and brought her baby to life. Its rumbling purr assured her the pair hadn't caused irreparable harm. The tobacco stench made her want to back over Cliff, but she checked over her shoulder before shifting into reverse. As soon as she lined up with the lane heading downtown, she gunned the engine, leaving a thin layer of rubber on the road as a reminder not to mess with her or her car.

At the first stoplight, she leaned across the gearshift and rolled down the passenger window to get rid of the cigarette stench, avoiding a peek at the back seat. "God, I don't even want to know if they screwed each other on your beautiful black leather, Barry. I swear I'll never let you out of my sight again."

A car honked behind her, and she barely stopped herself from flipping off the impatient prick. If Officer Hensley hadn't already given her a warning after the incident with the mayor's eighty-year-old mother-in-law, she would have.

Glaring at the shiny black pickup in the rearview mirror, she inched through the intersection and continued along High Street toward downtown in second gear. Its monstrous grill filled her back window the entire drive to Roma's Gourmet Gelato on the square. As she pulled into the diagonal space next to the curb, the tailgater angled in beside her. She slung her purse strap over her head and across her body, praying the owner of the pickup didn't open his big-ass door into her pride and joy.

The driver exited his vehicle and frowned at her through the open window. "It figures. If you don't know how to drive a stick, you should practice in a parking lot instead of backing up traffic on the road."

"Is this piss-off-the-short-tempered-Italian-chick day?" She shoved out of the car and slammed the heavy door shut. "Horns are for emergencies, jackass, and your truck would've been in my backseat if I'd needed to stop fast, so maybe *you* should practice *your* driving skills with Hot Wheels. And *it figures* better not have anything to do with my being female when you're obviously compensating for a tiny dick."

"I've never had any complaints about the size of my dick." Scowling at her over the top of Barry, the instigator buttoned his obviously tailored suit coat. Annoyance radiated through his dark sunglasses. It complemented his GQ-businessman beard stubble impeccably, making him exactly not her type. "I don't have time to argue with a crazy woman. I'm already running late because of you."

"Good, because I'd rather swim in a vat of used motor oil than waste a minute talking to an obnoxious twit whose most frequent sex partner is probably his hand. And keep your pathetic pecker in your pants around me or you'll be sorry." She sorted through her keys as she stepped onto the sidewalk and gave the chauvinistic loser her back. Between him and Cliff, they'd all but cured her of any craving for real sex, at least for today. She inserted the key into the deadbolt and twisted until the tumbler clicked into the unlock position. "I need more batteries and fewer men in my life."

The second lock stuck until she yanked upward on the door handle and tapped the lower corner of the door with the toe of her hiking boot. Although her actions probably looked like a frustrated effort to the casual observer, growing up with a locksmith father had taught her a few tricks to customize the security of the front door to her business.

"Need help?"

She blew out a noisy breath as she pushed inside. The last thing she needed was assistance from the alpha-tistical pig parked next to her. "Clearly not."

"You're Roma Denata?" His shadow, but not the swine himself, followed her through the doorway. "The *sweet* little ice-cream maker Glenn Frasier told me about?"

Whirling around to face the intruder, she positioned a key between her fingers as a makeshift weapon. *Glenn, you're getting a boot up the ass the next time I see you. I don't give a shit if you are my landlord.* "I'm not sweet and it's gelato, not ice cream. Everybody's little compared to your ego. State your business and go away."

The suit looked down at her and shook his head, but his perfectly mussed brown hair didn't budge. Amusement danced on his full kissable lips. "He didn't mention the chip on your shoulder is bigger than you are."

Smack-able, maybe, but not kissable. The fact that he was more than a foot taller than her and had rubbed her nose in it gave her reason enough to send him packing. "Fuck you."

His derisive snort added to her instant dislike of him. "I'm meeting Glenn here at eight, so if you want fucked, it'll have to be a quickie, little bit."

Behind him, a young woman walking a trio of shih tzus stared wide-eyed at Roma through the open door, having obviously overheard the most inappropriate part of tall-dark-and-arrogant's statement.

She wrenched the overgrown egomaniac inside, locked the door, and dragged him toward the kitchen. A flip of the switch flooded the work area in light. "Move it, buster."

At the sink, he planted his feet, preventing her from kicking him out the delivery entrance, and shoved his sunglasses into his hair. "You know I was just teasing you, right?"

"Were you now? I guess that makes you a pussy tease instead of a cock tease." *It doesn't feel so good when you're the target, does it?* She hooked her foot on the stepstool under the counter and slid it closer, ready to teach the spineless jerk a lesson. The second step brought her almost eye-to-eye with him. Then she hooked her arm around his neck and clamped her mouth on his.

He put up no resistance when she slid her tongue past his lips. Instead, he met her aggressive glide with one of his own. A low groan accompanied his attempt to take control, negating his claim that he hadn't meant what he said.

Typical male. She deepened the kiss and slipped her free hand beneath the back of his suit coat to palm his ass. The muscles tightened under her fingertips, encouraging her to continue her exploration. Pressing forward, she ground her pelvis against the growing lump in his pants. It was, by no measure, pathetic or tiny, but she wasn't about to give him the satisfaction of telling him so.

He groaned again as he guided her knee up to his hip and aligned the center seam of her cutoffs against his hard-on. The contact triggered a ripple of pleasure through her clit, stealing her breath and forcing a needy moan from her throat. A shudder spread through her insides and weakened her knees enough that she would've melted onto the floor if he hadn't had a hold of her.

Desperate for a breath, she pulled away. "Condom in my purse."

He froze, clearly shocked by her proposition, but his lust-clouded eyes outed his deepest desire. It matched hers—of that, she had no doubt.

She arched an eyebrow. "Unless you're too chicken to let me test-drive your tiny pathetic dick."

He rocked his hips into hers, evidently not willing to pass up her challenge. "I have one in my wallet."

His husky voice wound its way over her nerve endings and she worked his wallet free from his back pocket. She handed it to him as she lowered her foot to the stepstool. "Suit up."

While he freed his erection and rolled on the condom, she unfastened her shorts and pushed a single leg hole past her hiking boot, along with her underwear. Using the added height to her advantage, she draped her arms around his neck, hopped, and wrapped her legs around his waist.

He guided her onto his cock in a single smooth glide, stretching and filling her body all the way to her G-spot. Every movement as he carried her to the walk-in fridge behind her seated him deeper. "Still think I'm compensating?"

"Shut up and fuck me." She pressed her back to the metal door for leverage and arched toward him.

His mouth reconnected to hers and he thrust forward. Aggression clashed with her hunger, throwing her headlong into the beginnings of an orgasm, but he withdrew, stalling the release before it could fully develop. Then he lunged into her again, driving his tongue and his dick into her at the same time. Her spine ground into the unforgiving surface of the door. Once more, fireworks ignited without going off.

She growled into his mouth and dug her fingernails into his scalp, needing him to go faster and harder but unwilling to surrender in their battle of tongues to tell him. Bracing her shoulder blades against the metal, she tightened her thighs around him and met his next thrust halfway. The impact shattered the invisible barrier that had kept physical gratification out of her reach. Spots danced in her vision and tingles rushed through her limbs, carrying her up one mountainous peak after another. Rawness in her throat suggested her cries were long and loud, but his thunderous bellow drowned out the sound as he buried himself inside her with a last energetic shove.

His chest heaved in time with his panting and she let the erratic current of aftershocks race through her slack muscles. Leaning her head against the refrigerator door, she closed her eyes to enjoy the pulsing waves of post-orgasmic euphoria.

Holy Moses.

The buzz of the delivery entrance bell yanked her back to reality and she clutched at the stranger's lapels to keep from falling. "Put me down."

He lifted her off his still semi-hard cock in slow motion, triggering another tremor in her lower belly as he slid free. "Straighten your legs, short stuff."

Clenching her jaw, she removed her legs from his waist and waited for him to set her on the floor. Despite the wobbliness in her knees, she bent over to thread her boot through both right leg holes. "Call me that again, and you'll have a lip as fat as your ego."

He snickered as he tucked his sheathed dick in his pants and zipped up. "I'm pretty sure you'd need a ladder."

The buzzer rang again, interrupting her backswing to kick him in the shin.

"Better answer that." He pocketed his wallet and adjusted his tie.

Fairly certain the visitor was her landlord, based on the jerk's earlier comment, she ignored the doorbell and turned toward the cooler. "I'm not expecting anybody. Show yourself out when you tell whoever's there I said to go away. I'm busy and we're closed."

"Golly gee, I feel so used." He sneered through his smartass remark.

She shrugged as she entered the cold-storage unit for the pistachio mix she'd prepped last night. "The truth hurts sometimes. Don't let the door hit you in the ass on the way out."

Raucous laughter carried from the kitchen to the farthest set of shelving in the walk-in, where she hefted the container of milky drab-green liquid. A loud *thunk* announced his departure.

Alone at last. She waddled through the opening, ready to load the first batch in the churn.

"—met Roma then?" Glenn Frasier stood at the delivery entrance with the prick's outstretched hand in his. "Ah, Roma, how are you? I see you've met Lu—"

La la la la la. She screamed the repetitive phrase in her head to block out the intruder's name. A one-time fuck wasn't worthy of an introduction, especially when she had no plans to ever cross paths with him again.

"— new owner." Her landlord's grin warned her she'd missed something important.

She set the tub on the prep table and rubbed her palms over the ragged hem of her cutoffs. "What did you say?"

"Lucas here is the new owner of the building. Me and the missus are retiring to Florida."

"You sold the building without telling me?" Fury surged past the relative calm the orgasm had brought, and she grabbed the ladle hanging on the wall. "You. And you. *Fottutissimi stronzi, maledetti figli di puttana, fedifraghi bastardi, li mortacci vostri e chi non vi ci ha mai mandato! Fanculo! Tutti e due!*"

"Run!" Glenn bolted through the open service door.

Swinging her weapon, she chased his co-conspirator out after him. "*Giuro che vi taglio i coglioni e li do in pasto ai maiali!*"

CHAPTER 2

"Jesus, you told me she was sweet! Was that just a ploy to get me to buy the property?" Glad for the shade in the parking lot behind the gelato shop and its neighboring storefronts, Lucas Calloway slid his hand in his pocket to surreptitiously adjust the used condom pulling on his short hairs. Banshee was a more fitting description for Roma Denata, but his great uncle seemed to like the belligerent female. "And what the hell was she screeching at us?"

Glenn dabbed at his forehead with the wrinkled handkerchief he'd withdrawn from his plaid knee-length shorts. "Hoo-ey! I can't say for sure, but it was a doozy. Something about pig testicles, I think. She inherited more than a fierce temper from her *nonna*. Roma's got a knack for Italian insults like nobody's business. Watch out if she brings our ancestors into it, 'cause that means she's really ticked off."

"Temper, huh?" Maybe that explained her tendency to scream—when she was mad and when she had a rip-roaring orgasm. Lucas nodded toward the sidewalk leading between his properties and the next one. Disposing of the rubber was quickly becoming a top priority. "Come on, Uncle Glenn. I'll buy you a cup of coffee. I meant to grab one before our meeting, but I got stuck behind a slowpoke."

"Can't. I have an eight-thirty tee time. Gotta practice my putting first." Stuffing the handkerchief in his pocket, the older man grinned. "Give Roma a day or two to cool off before you talk to her again. Once she finds out you're honoring her lease, she'll be sweet as pie."

What's she going to be when I tell her she has to be out in thirty days? Lucas shook the old man's hand, not about to share that particular detail with his uncle or his tenant yet. "Thanks for the tip. Keep your head down and your eye on the ball."

"You bet." Glenn hurried toward Roma's Gourmet Gelato, the spring in his step a clear indication he was as happy to be free of the building as Lucas should've been to acquire it. Who could blame the old man for retiring when his renter seemed to have a perpetual lit fuse?

Taking the alley shortcut, Lucas headed for the coffee shop a block north of his truck. The condom had to go before it performed an unwanted bikini wax on him, and he could do with a dose of caffeine. He shouldn't have let the hotheaded pixie seduce him into screwing her brains out, but her fiery temperament turned him on as much as it irritated him. Besides, an early-morning fuck was never a bad thing, especially when it came with no strings.

He held the coffee shop door for a trio of thirty-something women in business attire as they exited, offering a roguish wink when the leggy redhead gave him an assessing once-over. They walked with their heads together, occasionally glancing back at him as they headed toward the crosswalk. Too bad the redhead had the look of a husband-hunter about her. His ego wasn't fat, even if it was well deserved.

An image of his new tenant in the throes of extraordinary orgasm popped into his mind as he stopped in the restroom to dispose of the Trojan and it stuck with him while he ordered a small black coffee to go. Although he rarely went back for seconds with the women he had sex with, he wouldn't be opposed to getting Roma Denata fully naked at least once. He hadn't gotten the opportunity to see, let alone touch, the overflowing handfuls filling out her form-fitting tank top. A glimpse at her probable double-D cleavage had sparked more than passing curiosity about what lay beneath the low-cut shirt. However, Uncle Glenn's timing would've been less than ideal if she'd taken time to strip off the rest of her clothes.

What's that saying he told me? Oh, yeah. Never fool around with a business associate unless you mean business. Fortunately, the gelato maker wouldn't be his business associate for long, and he never meant business in sexual liaisons. Relationships weren't part of his lifestyle.

With his jacket slung over his arm, he accepted his coffee from the barista and strolled toward the two newly vacant storefronts flanking his soon-to-be-displaced tenant. His plans for the space would finally appease his parents enough to stop their persistent badgering about his inability to settle down, although unwillingness was more accurate. The wife-and-kids thing held no appeal. He loved the freedom that came with being responsible for no one but himself—and picking up and moving on when the mood struck. Some men were better off living a life of nomadic bachelorhood.

"Luke? Luke Calloway?"

The impulse to pretend he hadn't heard someone calling his name almost propelled him back toward the coffee shop, as did pretending he wasn't Luke Calloway. Only somebody he'd grown up with in Wadsworth would know him by that name.

"It *is* you. I heard you were b-back in town." A wiry man in jeans, a T-shirt, and a John Deere cap popped out from behind a red pickup a few spots up from Lucas's truck as he crossed the street. Even with his eyes hidden behind sunglasses, the stranger was recognizable by his almost-cured stutter and every-stranger's-a-friend demeanor. "Word is you're staying for a while."

"Maybe. I haven't decided yet." At the curb, Lucas lost a fight with a smile and offered his hand to one of the few people who hadn't made his life a living hell until he was bigger and meaner than most of their classmates. "Bobby Vaughan, how have you been?"

After a quick swipe of his palm on his jeans, Bobby took Lucas's outstretched hand and gave it a robust shake. "Good. Real good. Been m-married ten years tomorrow, two kids, and I'm running my dad's pplumbing business since he retired. Can't complain at all. Roma tells me I'll be b-billing you now instead of Glenn for the work I'm doing. Says you bought him out so he can move to Florida. She was none too pleased about it, either."

Lucas shrugged and tossed his empty coffee cup in the trashcan outside the gelato shop. "She didn't know about the deal until this morning. Glenn didn't mention any problems with the plumbing. What's wrong?"

"Water heater needs replaced. Gotta be d-done by 'leven thirty when she opens."

Damn it. "You're sure it can't be repaired? How much?"

"Yup. It sprung a leak at the bottom out of the blue. Happens sometimes with old units. Wholesale plus labor. Where should I send the bill?"

"I'm setting up a temporary office next door. You can leave it in the mailbox by the back door."

"Will do." Bobby rapped his knuckles on the hood of his pickup and then climbed inside. "Gotta g-go pick up that new water heater. Call me and we'll have a beer sometime."

"You bet." The likelihood that his tenant had damaged the equipment to spite him almost convinced Lucas to face off with her again, but he waved at Bobby and walked to the space next door. Another round of angry sex wasn't on today's agenda.

Son of a bitch, I hope this property isn't a damn money pit.

He flipped through his ring of keys, determined to put Roma Denata and the plumbing problem out of his mind. Although he planned to locate a figurative escape hatch in case of emergency, a new opportunity lay on the other side of the door. The key turned, and the slight hitch of the moving deadbolt vibrated through his fingertips.

Pocketing his keys, he grasped the handle. The door didn't budge. A harder tug proved ineffectual. "Don't tell me I need to hire a locksmith too."

"Did you try lifting up on the handle and giving the lower right corner a nudge with your foot as you turn the key?" A woman's reflection stared back at him in the glass door. The dog sitting at her feet tilted its head, like it questioned his larger brain capacity. "It's a little trick to slow down burglars. I can show you how to do it if you like."

He did as she instructed and the door swung outward with a gentle pull. "That's what that kick and tug were about at the gelato shop. I thought the lock was stuck."

"You met Roma then?"

Careful to keep his body language neutral, he gave a curt nod.

Extending her hand, the woman smiled. Her companion eyed him with what looked like suspicion. She slackened the leash and the on-guard German shepherd seemed to relax. "Mr. Calloway, I'm Andria Kubicek, your nine o'clock appointment. And this is Maxine, my service dog. I know I'm early, but that's better than being late."

"I agree. Good to meet you, Andria. Call me Lucas." He shook her hand and then held the door open for her and her bodyguard. The dog seemed focused on the job, so he left her to it instead of greeting her. "Take your time looking around. Have you had a chance to review my proposal?"

"Several times. I have to say I'm a little surprised a successful businessman is interested in investing in something like this. You're not going to make money on it and you'll only be making a real difference in probably a few dozen lives. ROI and the bottom line seem important to you." Her perfunctory glances around the office space suggested she'd shown up for their meeting solely to be polite. "Nothing against the project or you. I'm just being honest."

"You're right." He slipped the slightly crumpled sample brochure from the inside pocket of his suit jacket and laid it on the built-in reception counter. Wild sex with his tenant hadn't done it any good. "I'm partnering with a foundation that supports the local rape-crisis line and a safe-house. They want to expand to include recovery services, a low-cost self-defense studio, and a couple other projects that are still in the idea stage. Your personal experience and professional background make you the perfect person to run the recovery services office."

She took the brochure he offered as she walked past the reception area and toward the meeting rooms. "It's a nice space. Plenty of room for individual and group therapy, workshops, support group sessions. Do you have a list for legal and outside psychotherapy referrals? Or would that be one of my responsibilities?"

"The Foundation has someone who's handling the referral list. They want you to develop a plan for the kinds of services we should provide to clients, hire staff, and manage the office once it's up and running. There are two large meeting rooms upstairs, but we can modify the space to make better use of it, if necessary."

Stopping outside the conference room, she looked at him over her shoulder, holding his gaze long enough to set his nerves on edge. "You're obviously aware that I'm a rape survivor. If you don't mind my asking, what's your connection? Why are you invested in this project?"

He caught his jaw tightening and made a conscious effort to loosen the muscles. "A member of my family was raped. My parents started the Foundation several years ago to provide resources she didn't have access to."

The words he'd practiced for hours on end the last few weeks were only marginally easier than the first time he'd said them aloud.

"I'm glad they created something positive from such a horrible thing." She turned away, freeing him from the same haunted look he recognized from family gatherings. "They say everybody knows someone who's been affected by it."

"Yes." Having sat through a presentation on current rape statistics during the most recent Foundation meeting, he hoped Andria didn't plan to further educate him on the subject.

Thankfully, she was quiet as she explored the rest of the two-story building with her watchful companion.

The *click, click, click* of the dog's toenails on the wood stairs announced their return to the first floor five minutes later. As Andria rounded the newel post, she locked onto his gaze again. "What's the next step if I decide I'm interested in the position? Do you have other interviews lined up?"

Lucas pushed away from the reception counter where he'd waited during her self-guided tour. "Although I'm acting only as a liaison for the Foundation, I've been asked to make a hiring recommendation from a list they provided because of my business expertise. Out of the five potential candidates, I believe you're the best qualified for the job and I've already made the Board aware of my choice. Unless you're not interested, I don't see the point in meeting with any of the others."

Nothing about her serious expression gave away her thoughts. "You seem pretty confident about my abilities, even though you haven't even seen my official resume."

"I had a name. An unusual one, at that. A little online research can produce a decent profile when you know where to look. Being local also helped." He gestured for her to lead the way to the exit and followed her outside. "Thanks for meeting with me. I'd like to have an answer on Monday. You have my contact information if you have any questions."

She nodded and adjusted her hold on the leash. "I'll be in touch in a day or two. I have some things to think about."

"Of course. You're welcome to take the full four days if you need them."

The dog fell into step beside her as she nodded again and headed in the opposite direction of the gelato shop. Her steady gait exuded an air of subtle confidence and determination, not at all what he would've expected from a woman whose life had exploded four years ago. The violation of her body and the unfortunate demise of her marriage hadn't broken her. She was strong and brave—a survivor. That's why he'd chosen her to lead others through recovery. His gut was seldom wrong.

He shoved the key in the lock, crossing his fingers that securing the door didn't require another secret handshake. The lower bolt clicked into place, but numerous tries with the upper mechanism failed until he yanked the handle upward and gave the door a none-too-gentle kick.

Security measure or not, the glitchy deadbolts have to go.

His cell buzzed against his palm as he typed in "call a locksmith" to his growing to-do list. The name and number triggered a mix of affection and agitation. He bulldozed through the disconcerting feelings and tapped the Answer button. "Hi, Mom."

"G'morning, sunshine. How did it go?" Metal clinked against glass and birds chirped in the background, confirming his mother sat on the deck with her usual endless pot of morning tea while she reviewed Foundation paperwork.

He cast a frown toward the building to his left as he walked to his truck. "My tenant cussed out Uncle Glenn and me in Italian while she was swinging a ladle and chasing us out the door. I also have to pay for a new water heater and all the exterior locks need replaced."

Boisterous laughter forced him to move the phone away from his ear and switch to speaker. When he slid behind the steering wheel, it finally quieted.

"You've met Roma then. Actually, I was wondering how your meeting with Andria went."

Heat crept up his neck with her observation. Why had his thoughts immediately gone to Roma Denata? "Fine. She promised to give me an answer by Monday."

"Do you think she'll accept the offer?"

"Maybe? I don't know. She said she had to think about it." His usual ability to read people hadn't worked on her, but he'd also been distracted by the woman next door.

"That's better than an outright no. I'm sure it's a hard decision. She's welcome to call me if she has questions or concerns."

"I'll let her know." He fastened his seatbelt and started the engine. "Tell Dad I said hi."

Her lengthy silence assured him she recognized his attempt to cut the call short. "I will. Are you free for supper tomorrow?"

Yes.

No.

Glancing in the rearview mirror, he scrambled for an excuse. The front end of Bobby's red truck filled the reflection and saved him from the family meal he'd managed to avoid for nearly a week. "Sorry, I can't tomorrow night. I ran into an old friend from school and we're supposed to meet up for a beer. Sometime later this weekend might work, though."

"Okay. Talk to you soon. I love you."

"I love you too." He shifted into reverse as he ended the call. Guilt churned in his gut from the white lie and her obvious awareness of it, but that was life.

CHAPTER 3

"Damn it." Roma fished the last piece of eggshell from the flour-sugar mixture and flicked it into the food-waste bucket. In fifteen years of making waffle cones and bowls, she'd never dropped a shell in the batter—until now.

Damn you, Calloway, and your stupid dick too.

The egomaniac's presence had met her at the delivery entrance bright and early this morning and refused to get the hell out of her kitchen and her mind. Even using the stepstool to reach the case of gelato spoons in the supply room had triggered a gasp-inducing contraction in her lower belly.

She wiped her messy fingers on the cleaning towel and set the mixer dial to the Beat setting. The yolks whirled through the beaters and burst, shooting long streaks of bright yellow goo into the batter like a jizz-spewing male orgasm. The only thing missing was a satisfied roar to signal the release.

That is seriously fucked up. But damned if yesterday's hit-and-run hadn't scratched the itch she'd been fighting for months.

She drizzled vanilla and melted butter into the creamy mixture, determined to banish the incident and the prick from her thoughts. The number of items on her to-do list before she opened the shop wasn't getting any shorter.

Short. Grr. That word will no longer be a part of my vocabulary.

Her list was big, long, and massive.

She shut off the mixer, stomped into the walk-in cooler, and let out a therapeutic screech. Why did everything remind her of her new landlord's cock when she'd made a point of not even looking at it?

God, she had felt it, though. *Deep, hard, and filling.*

Another vicious growl did nothing to drive the memory from her body.

"Roma?" The muffled greeting announced the arrival of Tess, one of her part-timers. "Are you in there? You okay?"

Grabbing a bag of melt-able chocolate wafers and another of vanilla chips from the closest shelf, she pushed open the insulated door—the same one that had left a friction burn on her shoulder blade yesterday. "Morning, Tess. I'll be fine until I have to deal with another asshole."

The younger woman snickered and tucked a few strands of white-blonde hair behind her ear. "Good luck with that. Do you want me to make the cones or plug and dip?"

"Neither." Roma tossed her helper the wafers on her way to the counter. "I want you to convince me that eating pussy is better than fucking and sucking cock."

A contemptuous snort accompanied Tess's fake scowl. "If I have to convince you to enjoy dining out, you're not in the closet and no amount of willpower can put you there. What's the matter? Did you accidentally screw another guy who wants to date you?"

Roma barked out a laugh. "That would be a no. He despises me as much as I despise him. I'd stake my sex life on it."

"Wow. That's pretty sure. But the physical chemistry was phenomenal, right?"

"Maybe." As the waffle cone maker preheated, Roma gathered the batter scoops, tongs, and forming tools to keep from reliving the episode in her mind for the hundredth time. "It would've been better if he'd been gagged. Men really need to learn to keep their mouths shut, especially before and after sex."

Tess dumped the wafers into the top of one double boiler and switched on the hotplate. She paused with the vanilla chips poised above the other melting pot. "Hmm. You know, part of the turn-on could be that you don't like each other and there's zero chance of a long-term relationship. Or it could be you're both into mutually satisfying angry sex. What do you have to be mad at him about? Why's he mad at you?"

"He's rude, misogynistic, and obnoxious. I seriously doubt if he cared whether I got off or not. And more than likely, he's pissed off because I'm smarter than he is."

"Because you're a smart ass, you mean." A chuckle mingled with the plink of chips in the pan. "By the way, that's a compliment, in case you were wondering."

"Of course I'm a smart ass, but I'm also smarter than he is." Roma spread a small scoopful of batter on the left griddle and closed the lid. Then she repeated the process with the larger scoop on the right. "Speaking of smart, did you hear back about any of the internships you interviewed for?"

"Yep." Tess's broad smile brightened the room. "Three offers, including my first choice."

"Good job!" Roma peeled the first waffle from the griddle and used a clean flour-sack towel to mold it around the smaller cone form. "Hands-free high five."

"High ten back atcha. Thanks for writing a reference letter. And the job. And letting me work around my class schedules."

"You're welcome, but I'll fire your ass if you go around telling people I'm nice." After adding batter to the empty griddle, Roma removed and shaped the bigger waffle.

The young woman rolled her eyes and stuck out her tongue. "I didn't say you were nice. You broke my heart when you told me you prefer real dicks to strap-ons."

Not even trying to fight her laughter as she closed the refilled waffle iron, Roma flipped her middle finger in Tess's direction. "Don't knock cock 'til you try it. Besides, I'm old enough to be your mother."

"True. You already have one foot in the grave with the big four-oh coming up next week. Does your fuckbuddy know how old you are?"

Roma shrugged and rolled another cone. "I'm not having sex with him again, so who cares?"

"What if you change your mind? It *was* phenomenal sex, and you can be prepared with a gag next time. There's a lot to be said for knowing what to expect."

"Not happening. Once is definitely my limit with this particular jerk-wad." More wisps of steam rose from the waffle maker, filling the air with its delicious vanilla scent. "Can you run two cans of whipped cream out to the mini fridge while you're waiting for the candy to melt? Oh, and grab the cocoa, will you? I promised *Nonna* I'd have chocolate cones and bowls for the Book Club Bandits' meeting this afternoon."

"You just want to change the subject because the guy has you all hot and bothered, and you don't like it one bit. Do you want chocolate or vanilla dips and plugs for the chocolate cones?" Tess's short skirt flounced upward as she spun toward the walk-in, revealing her pert bike-shorts-clad butt.

And it doesn't do a goddamn thing for me. "Chocolate. Wait a sec. She wanted to know if I could get cannabis-laced chocolate. I didn't have the heart to tell her no, so I mixed some dried oregano and parsley. Add about a quarter teaspoon or so and let me taste it. Here, sprinkle it in." Gesturing to the baggie of herbs near the hot plate, Roma grinned.

"You better hope she doesn't find out."

"She won't unless one of us tells her, and I'm not going to."

"Fine, I'll keep my mouth shut." Tess disappeared into the supply closet and emerged again with the container of unsweetened cocoa powder. "What're today's specials? I'll go ahead and put the sign in the window while I'm out front."

"Amaretto, peach, and stracciatella."

Roma continued her spread, peel, and roll process while her helper retrieved the whipped cream from the cooler and headed to the serving counter to take care of the next two items on the daily to-do list. The repetitive motions allowed her thoughts to wander back to yesterday's quickie again, with the added scents of melting chocolate and warm vanilla amplifying the orgasmic memory. While she had no interest in fucking Lucas a second time, remembering the pleasure his cock had given her would make for good masturbation inspiration.

Hmm. Maybe I can run home for a session with—

"Do you have a minute, Roma?" Her sister stood in the kitchen doorway, hands clasped in front of her and her bottom lip caught between her teeth.

Whose ass do I need to kick? "Sure. Come on in. Do you mind if I keep working? I need to finish this batch before we open."

Andria took two steps into the room and stopped. "I just wanted to let you know I'll be gone this weekend. A friend asked me to house sit."

The towel slipped as Roma pressed the waffle around the form. "Shit! That's hot. If I didn't know better, I'd say you don't like living with me anymore. This is the third overnighter in the last month."

"Of course I like living at your house." Looking down toward her feet, Andria sighed. "I don't know what I would've done without you after…"

Roma's stomach twisted into a tangled mess around the cold calzone she'd scarfed down for breakfast. "I'm sorry. Forget I said anything. Not enough coffee this morning. Just let me know when you get there, okay? And check in once in a while?"

Her sister nodded. "I will. See you Sunday evening."

"Yep." Willing away the churning in her gut, Roma lifted the lid to remove another waffle. The wafting steam added to her nausea, and she turned away to suck in a cool breath.

Andria still stood in the doorway, looking like she had something more on her mind. "I… Never mind. You have work to do and it can wait. Talk to you later."

Before Roma could respond, her little sister was gone.

Concern niggled at her as she prepared enough cones and bowls to last through the eleven-thirty-to-one rush and transferred the gelato-filled serving pans to the freezer case. Even when she raised the blinds and unlocked the entrance, questions circled in her head.

Was Andria trying to hide from someone who'd made her uncomfortable?

If Maxine doesn't tear his balls off, I will.

Or had the job interview she'd mentioned last week become a job offer?

What if she'd met a man and was considering going out with him?

The last speculation triggered the most anxiety. No matter how well a woman thought she knew a guy, he always had secrets—the kind that could destroy lives. She barely conquered a swell of panic before her first customers of the day walked in from what seemed to be the beginning of another sweltering July day.

The younger of the two boys slipped free of his male guardian's grasp and ran to the counter. Only the top of his curly-haired head was visible until he climbed onto the kid shelf she'd installed years ago. "Hurry, Daddy. I'm hot. I need gelly."

She peeked at him through the case and waved. "What'll it be today, Brayden?"

He pressed his finger to the glass, leaving little smudges. "That one."

"Can you read the label to me?"

"Strack-a. Strack-a-tella."

"Good try. You can almost speak Italian. The *c* and the *i* make sort of a *ch* sound." With a plastic bowl at the ready, she slid the door open and grabbed a scoop. "Do you want a rocket or a clown this time?"

"A rocket! With lots of smoke!"

"You got it. Go sit down at a table while I put it together." She placed the scoop of vanilla laced with bits of chocolate in the bowl and topped it with a small waffle cone, point side straight up. As she squirted whipped cream around the base, she grinned at Brayden's older brother. "The usual, Bryce?"

"Yes, Miss Roma. Thank you." He joined Brayden at the table in the corner, leaving her alone with their cute but stuffy father.

Ben stepped up to the counter, not a hint of five-o'clock shadow on his jaw or a wrinkle in his short-sleeved button-up shirt to mar his single-father-looking-for-an-appropriate-wife image. "A scoop of vanilla bean in a cup please."

Suppressing an eye roll and an "obviously," she nodded. "I'll have those ready for you in a jiffy. Tess'll take care of you at the register."

Instead of moving down the counter to the checkout stand, he leaned in and lowered his voice. "You're terrific with the boys. They talk about you all the time."

"They're good kids." She scraped the scoop across the top of the strawberry, filling it to the edge and then using a second scoop to do the same with mint. A little careful maneuvering ended with a bi-color gelato ball in a small waffle bowl. She added a red spoon and stood a blue one in Brayden's "smoke."

"Would you have a late dinner with me tomorrow night? They're going to my parents' for the weekend."

Mr. Divorced Attorney wants a little action, does he? After a quick scoop rinse in the bucket, she dipped his boring vanilla into its boring cup and added a boring white spoon. "You're my lawyer, Ben. Companionship, a booty call, or whatever it is you're looking for isn't happening."

"I didn't mean…" A blush the color of his older son's gelato crept up his neck. "I don't want a one-night stand."

"Yeah, well, that's all I want. I hear the new orthodontist is in the market for a husband. Smart. Pretty. Redhead." She carried the tray with his order to the end of the counter and made eye contact with the trio of women entering the shop. "There she is now. Introduce yourself."

The dentist's gaze veered to the left as she passed the tables, clearly zooming in on Ben. At the counter, she finally looked in Roma's direction again. "I'd like a scoop of vanilla bean in a cup please."

Roma cleared her throat to keep from laughing her head off. "Ready in a sec. Pick up is down at the register. By the way, his name is Ben Kaiser and he's available." *Ben, I deserve a year's free retainer for this.*

The woman's flawless smile broadened. "He is? Thanks for the tip."

"Don't mention it." Roma handed off the order to Tess. "Next!"

A steady line kept her busy long after Ben and his boys followed the redhead outside, but the arrival of *Nonna* and the Book Club Bandits at one forty-five promised a truly effective distraction. The ladies from the senior condo community gathered at the counter, their chatter encompassing everything from this week's book and today's flavors to the hot pool guy and the hunky lawn-care crew.

"Two scoops of my favorite espresso, *tigrotta*." Her grandmother hobbled forward with her cane and then aimed it at the stack of chocolate waffle bowls on the counter beside the freezer case. "In one of those *fancy* edible dishes."

"Coming right up, *Nonna*." *Save my soul from the devil for lying to you.* "How's your knee?"

"Better soon. The doctor says to rest. I tell her I don't have time to waste on sitting." The old woman frowned. "Sit too long and you don't get up."

"I don't think either of us has to worry about that, but you should eat at a table like a civilized person." Roma added a second scoop of the fragrant latté-brown gelato to the cannabis-free bowl. "I'll bring it out to you."

Nonna nodded, evidently pacified by the recitation of her most common admonishment from Roma's childhood. "You make me proud."

Halfway around the end of the counter with her delivery, Roma stopped short when a wide-eyed Tess pointed toward the front entrance. "A guy in a suit wants to talk to you. And, damn, does he have a presence."

Piss off, Calloway. "Tell him to make an appointment."

Tess scrunched up her nose. "I told him you were busy with a private party, but he said it's important and to meet him next door in five minutes. Then he left."

"Presumptuous ass. Let's get everybody served. And no rushing." Resuming her delivery, Roma wove through the crowd of Bandits waiting for their afternoon treat.

He can damn well wait until I'm good and ready.

CHAPTER 4

Eight more minutes had passed, but Lucas reread the email on his laptop screen for the fourth time and loosened his tie instead of letting Roma Denata's tardiness chew on his last nerve. The CLOSED FOR PRIVATE PARTY 1:45 TO 3:00 sign might make an acceptable reason, if not for the fact that she'd likely use any excuse to make him wait.

His phone buzzed against the desk, shooting his pulse into high gear. No name came up with the unfamiliar number, but it was local. "Hello, this is Lucas Calloway."

"Mr. Calloway. Lucas. This is Andria Kubicek. I'd like more information."

Leaning back in his chair, he switched from speaker to ear. "Good to hear from you, Andria. I'll be happy to answer your questions if I can. If not, I'll find out. What would you like to know?"

"I'm concerned about security at the center. Do you have a plan for protecting clients and the staff?"

He minimized the browser window and clicked on the file with the proposal, brochure, and his notes. "A security system, including cameras and coded locks, is scheduled to be installed in less than two weeks—after we finalize the floor plan. Sign in and sign out at the reception desk. IDs checked for everyone who enters the building. Emergency and lockdown procedures. It's modeled after the most secure facilities of this type and the Foundation contracted a security expert for consultation through the entire process. That includes background checks on all employees and volunteers. I can email you the list of precautions the Board discussed and you're welcome to make additional suggestions."

"I'd appreciate it. Being safe is as important as having access to counseling and other resources."

"Absolutely. I'm sending the document right now. Is there anything else I can do to help with your decision?"

She was silent for several seconds, as if weighing whether or not to ask her next question. "My husband and I are reconciling and I want to discuss the job offer with him. Is it okay if I tell him your name and some details about the job? Oh, and I'd rather you didn't share this. We haven't told anyone yet."

The hope in her voice was enough to make him root for her and her ex. They deserved a happier ending than they'd gotten four years ago.

He clicked the Send button. "Not a problem and I'll consider our conversation confidential. Don't hesitate to get in touch if you have other questions."

"Thank you. I'll have an answer for you soon."

"You're welcome. Have a good weekend." As he ended the call, the clock on his phone reminded him how much time had passed since his request that Roma meet with him—more than half an hour. He tapped his pen on the desk, counting off another fifteen seconds. "Spiteful woman."

"Usually." Roma stood framed by the doorway to the smallest conference room he'd temporarily commandeered. This time, her raggedy cutoffs were paired with a fire-engine-red tank top and matching high tops. For as petite as she was, her toned legs seemed to go on for miles. Their previous encounter had proven they were definitely long enough to wrap around his hips for a ride. "You have ten minutes."

His pulse, his dick, and the itch for a battle snapped to attention.

How the hell did she sneak in without me noticing? "It only took me about thirty seconds to make you come yesterday. You're late."

"You took thirty seconds to make *yourself* come. Good thing *I* made sure my orgasm happened before you got your rocks off." She sauntered across the room and plopped her shapely ass on the edge of the desk. Her bare thigh tempted him to run his fingers from her knee to the tattered hem of her shorts. Then she leaned toward him, giving him a mouthwatering view of her cleavage. "Nine minutes and forty-five seconds."

Her challenging tone zipped straight to his balls. Did she really believe he didn't give a damn if his partners got any enjoyment out of sex?

"Tick tock, Mr. Calloway."

Some pleasure before business? The expanding hard-on in his pants struggled for freedom as he stood. Thankfully, he'd had the foresight to replace the condom they'd used from his wallet yesterday. "I can last longer if you want me to, but limiting me to nine minutes and however-many seconds puts constraints on what I can do. How about multiple orgasms this time?"

"For you or me?" Her nipples poked at the thin fabric, exposing her interest, even more than the huskiness in her voice.

Not bothering to hide a laugh, he slipped his wallet from his back pocket and fished out the condom. "That sounds like a challenge, short stuff."

She spun her perfect butt on the desk, stopping with one arm braced behind her and a high top resting against his zipper. Then she grabbed him by the tie and tugged. "Unless you want this thing stuffed in your mouth, I suggest you stop calling me that and make me come. Multiple times."

He rocked his hips forward, increasing the pressure on his cock and using her foot to hold him upright as he closed his hand over her breast. His breath caught in his throat, but he managed to swallow a needy moan. A flick across her taut nipple and a firm caress along the crotch seam of her shorts drew a whimper. He paused above the intersection of vertical and horizontal seams and pressed harder for several seconds.

Her lips parted and her head fell back as she cried out. Then visible spasms rippled through the muscles beneath her tank top.

Holy hell, that was fast. One down. At least one more to go. He bent forward to kiss her knee. "Undress while I suit up. I want you naked."

"Not expecting visitors this time, are you?" She swung away as fast as she'd pivoted toward him and hopped off the desk.

"No." Glad he'd shed his suit coat after a lunch meeting with the couple he'd identified to run the self-defense studio, he kicked off his shoes.

Her shorts slid down her legs with a shimmy of her hips, leaving a red lace thong that revealed far more than it covered. She crossed her arms and grasped the hem of her shirt. "Good, because I locked the door behind me."

He stalled with his pants around his ankles, mesmerized by the no-nonsense way she stripped. Not a hint of self-consciousness or embarrassment showed in the smooth glide of fabric past the curls escaping the messy knot on top of her head. More red lace cupped her breasts until she peeled it from her body as well. He licked his lips, tempted by the two generous mounds of pale flesh topped with peaks the color of creamy milk chocolate.

"What? You've never seen a pair of tatas before?" She added the thong to the pile of her clothing on the floor, giving him a spectacular view of her ass.

"Appreciating a work of art. Lean, strong, and curves in all the right places."

"Well, I'm just here for the sex. Appreciate on your own damn time." Picking up the condom, she raised one eyebrow. "Kind of hard to dress your dick for the party with your Jockeys on."

He shoved his boxer briefs downward and stepped out of both items ringing his ankles. His balls tightened at her scrutiny, inciting a distinctly pleasant sensation. "Do you want to do the honors?"

"Honors?" She scowled and tossed the packet at him across the desk. "It's a dick, not a bottle of champagne. Put on the raincoat or I'm outta here."

Her disinterest in foreplay, civilized conversation, or a relationship in order to have sex put her in a category apart from most women, not that he minded. Her expectations seemed to match his—physical release and nothing more. However, the way her gaze shifted from above his neck to somewhere below his waist assured him she liked what she saw.

He tore open the foil package and rolled on the protection. "Oral, manual, or intercourse for your next orgasm?"

She rounded the desk and stopped an arm's length from him. "Fucked. Unbutton your shirt and sit in the chair."

Somehow, her bossy tone turned him on as much as it irritated him. Actually, that was a lie. Anticipation far outweighed annoyance. He slipped one button after another free in quick succession, yanked his loosened-but-still-knotted tie over his head, and discarded his shirt. The leather seat was cool against his skin, but only one thing could put out the fire spreading through his insides. "How much time do I have left?"

"Eight minutes." She placed her right knee next to his thigh and straddled him in a smooth motion. Before he could take a preparatory breath, she sank onto his cock.

A groan exploded from his chest and he squeezed the padded arms to keep from blowing his claim that he could last as long as she wanted. Her pussy closed around him, hugging his dick like she planned to hold him hostage for at least the rest of the day.

Then she lowered her mouth to his, diving between his lips as she ran her fingertips from his shoulders to his ribs. Her kiss embodied every bit of the aggression she'd aimed at him during her temperamental Italian spectacle.

She traced circles around his pecs and an unexpected jolt shot to his cock when she pinched his nipples. The contrast of pleasure and pain almost pushed him to the edge, but the awareness that she wouldn't let him live down a premature ejaculation helped him hold on by a thread.

Two can play at that game, you little nymph.

Reaching around her, he flattened a palm against her back and pulled her close enough that her tight buds brushed his chest. With his other hand gripping her butt cheek, he ground himself deeper. A groan escaped him, but hers became a muffled cry. Her muscles pulsed and convulsed around him, trying like hell to drag him along for the ride.

One more for the road.

He rocked upward, meeting her halfway and sliding deeper still. As he synchronized their in-and-out rhythm with their kiss, she arched against him, fighting him for control every step of the way. His balls tightened, but he growled and thrust into her again, determined to force her across the finish line first.

Her fingernails dug into his skin and her pussy clutched him tighter than before. She broke away from his mouth, her high-pitched keening signaling him to give in to the heat rushing up his length. She gasped as he buried himself inside her a last time and voiced his satisfaction through the flashing colors.

His throat ached, but every other part of his body floated in the sublime afterglow of amazing sex. "By my count…that was…three. With about…that many minutes left. Want more?"

She scrambled off of him, her lunge for the desk a clear indication her equilibrium was as shot to hell as his. Wobbly legs carried her to the other side, where she yanked on her clothes. Without looking back, she exited his office and then the rear door banged shut.

A discussion about his changes to the lease agreement would evidently have to wait until tomorrow or Sunday. Maybe by then he could handle being in the same room with her—without an instantaneous hard-on short-circuiting his brain.

Struggling against his own lack of coordination, he reached for his underwear and pants. After a search through his desk drawers, he removed the used condom and wrapped it in a spare napkin. At least he wouldn't have to suffer through accidental hair removal today.

His phone vibrated on the desk as he slid the knot of his tie toward his collar a few minutes later. The name and number triggered the same mix of emotions it always did, but guilt was lower on the balance since he'd made arrangements to meet Bobby for a beer later.

"Hi, Mom." He tucked his wallet in his back pocket and paced to the outer reception area, away from the lingering scent of his distracting tenant and sex.

"Hi, Lucas. Have you heard from Andria? I know it's probably too soon for an answer, but I'd love to get started on the center as soon as possible."

"She called a little while ago, wanting to know more about what kind of security we'll have. I sent her the notes from our meeting with the consultant." His reflection stared back at him in the wall of glass facing the street. Longer-than-usual hair and a week's worth of scruff made the man in the mirror look more like a thug than a businessman. "She said she'd get back to me soon."

"Good. I knew asking you to review and interview candidates was the right thing to do. Thank you for coming home to help with this project. It means a lot to me."

The words she didn't say could've filled the Taj Majal, amplifying the guilt that never went away. He gave the glass his back and paced to the opposite end of the rental space. "I'm headed to the office in a couple minutes for a meeting with the budget director. Do you need anything?"

"You're at the building, aren't you?"

The reminder that he'd refused a workspace at the Foundation in favor of someplace more private added to his self-reproach. "Yeah. I had to take some measurements for the contractor."

"Would you mind stopping next door for a scoop of mint gelato?"

"The shop's closed for a private party."

"Oh, I forgot today's Friday. The book club meets there once a week. How about a smile and a hug instead?"

"Are you sure I won't be interrupting your work on the fundraiser?" He returned to the office for his computer bag and to turn off the lights.

"Yes, I'm sure. The committee has everything under control and you're always welcome to interrupt what I'm doing, just like when you were two and seven and fourteen. Nothing is more important than the people I love."

And the guilt trip turns into a month-long expedition. "Okay. I'll be there by three. Gotta go." He ended the call and walked to the front of the building, even though he'd parked in the rear lot.

After a stop at the florist two blocks up the street, he followed the sidewalk to the alley and to the parking lot with the offering for his mother. She would thank him for the armful of daisies and he would play the good son until he left town again.

CHAPTER 5

"Go. I'll finish closing up." Roma set the pile of the drippy serving pans in the sink, wishing she could heave every last one of them at the wall.

Tess frowned as she adjusted her purse strap across her body at the back door. "Okay. See you tomorrow."

A grunt was all Roma could manage after holding her temper all day. She'd waited and waited to cuss out her worthless piece of shit of a landlord for cheating on his girlfriend with her.

Yeah, I saw you with those daisies, you unfaithful prick.

Screwing for sex was fine, but she wanted no part of that kind of scheme. Men were such pigs—fucking one woman while giving another flowers. Evidently, three orgasms for "the other woman" earned the cheater's victim a giant bouquet.

She turned the hot-water faucet on full blast and stalked to the freezer case for the bucket of scoops. "*Fottutissimo stronzo.*"

Clanking the metal pans and utensils in the soapy water brought no relief from the anger simmering in her veins. Only a good fuck—not happening—or an Italian rant at the target of her rage would vent the steam that had been building since yesterday afternoon.

With the dishes draining, the floor mopped, and the counters wiped, she dragged and kicked a trio of empty boxes from the storeroom to the service entrance and out the door. A well-aimed punch broke through the bottom of the first cardboard case with a satisfying *pop*. She stomped it flat and then hefted it into the recycle bin.

"Who pissed you off this time?"

The urge to take a swing at the prick behind her won out over the tiny part of her that wanted to ignore Lucas Calloway. Her fist connected with air when he jumped back. "You lousy excuse for a human being."

His shady grin shone bright under the streetlight. "Me again? What did I do now?"

"As if you didn't know, you swine." She throttled the second box and trampled it into a manageable rectangle. "Does your girlfriend know you've been cheating on her?"

"*Girlfriend?*" The horror in his voice made her pause with the cardboard halfway in the bin. His mouth contorted into a disgusted grimace. "I don't have a girlfriend, and that includes you."

"Who said I wanted to be your girlfriend? Just a tad bit arrogant with your assumptions, Calloway."

"And I wouldn't cheat if I did."

She gave the cardboard a shove and turned to face the bald-faced liar. "Really? So you had desk sex with me and bought yourself flowers ten minutes later?"

Egotistical laughter echoed off the brick walls and through the parking lot. "They were for my mother. Maybe you should be more careful about *your* assumptions, short stuff. Or are you mad because I didn't buy them for you? Three orgasms *and* daisies seem kind of excessive for someone who isn't my girlfriend, don't you think?"

A laugh at her expense, she could live with, but throwing that damn moniker at her again crossed the line. She balled up her fist and socked him in the bicep. "Your arrogance is astounding. Why are you here anyway?"

He rubbed the spot and lapsed into silence for a full minute. "I'm horny and you're handy."

"Wow, you really have a way with words, King Kong. That

certainly explains why you don't have a girlfriend." She stomped through the final box and disposed of it. "You might try something like 'I'm horny and sex with you is better than average.' It'll improve your chances of getting laid. Otherwise, you can be *handy* all by yourself."

"I'm horny for *you*." His taut jaw and unreadable expression suggested he wasn't pleased about it. "Because the sex is a hell of a lot better than average."

The husky admission settled in her lower belly, pinging back and forth between her vaginal and uterine muscles. "Ah, hell. Meet me at my car in two minutes."

Before he could open his mouth and ruin the moment, she hurried inside to switch off the lights and lock up. A final check of the front entrance, the walk-in cooler door, and the faucets brought her to the tiny office, where she twisted the dial on the safe and grabbed her purse. Keys in hand, she exited the shop.

Three spaces from top-down Barry, Lucas stood at the rear bumper of his truck with his hands stuffed in the pockets of his shorts and his ankles crossed above his running shoes. As she approached her car, he pushed away from the tailgate and closed the distance between them. "Do you want to follow me to my place? Or should I follow you to yours?"

She tossed her purse on the 'Cuda's passenger seat and climbed in the back. "Right here. Right now."

"My backseat's bigger. And it has a roof."

"Sky looks clear to me. Afraid the neighbors will catch us?"

"No, the whole town." He combed his fingers through his hair, giving him a just-rolled-out-of-bed style. "We tend to get kind of loud."

Kneeling on the bench seat, she unfastened her cutoffs. "I can be quiet."

His eyebrows shot up and he gave her a doubtful look. "I'll believe that when I see it."

"Climb in and I'll prove it." She wiggled out of her shorts and undies, hoping to entice him inside. "I'm ready."

"I know I'm going to regret this."

"Performance anxiety?"

"Hardly. Cramped space. You should be on top so I don't squish you." He hopped into the backseat and dug a condom from his pocket. In record time, his erection was free and covered in latex. Before she could squeeze between the front bucket seats to give him room, he picked her up by the waist and stretched out on the bench seat. With his head propped against the interior side molding and his legs folded into the legroom behind the driver's seat, he lowered her onto his lap. "Slide your top up so I can suck while you fuck."

Heat flooded her pussy at his demand. She complied, and an adjustment to her position put her over his stiff cock. A long, slow glide down his length nearly pushed a moan from her throat, but she had to bite the inside of her cheek to keep from crying out when his mouth closed on her breast. A flick of his tongue on her nipple sparked a warning tremor. "Fuck, fuck, fuck."

"Mmm." He thumbed her other nipple and a finger found her clit as he rocked his hips up to meet her pelvis.

Pleasure ricocheted through her body, making her abs vibrate, and she slapped her hand over her mouth to hold in the scream that wanted out.

Lust gleamed in his eyes and his lips curved upward against her breast. Then he wiggled his cock inside her. Clearly, he intended to try to match or exceed his high score for orgasms.

Challenge accepted. She braced her hands on his chest and set a rhythm sure to get him off.

"Car." His choked whisper only added to her determination to beat him at his own game.

"They're welcome to watch." She panted through the onslaught of excitement, from the possibility of being caught and the upward swing toward another release.

His dick swelled, filling her completely as headlights flashed across the windshield. "Jesus, I'm gonna come."

Unable to slow the avalanche about to bury her in sexual madness, she clutched at his shirt and covered his mouth with hers. He bucked into her, his stifled groan smothering her breathless cry. Tingles skittered to her fingers and toes as peak after peak carried her along an almost endless journey of gratification.

His kiss softened with the tension in his body until the spots in her peripheral vision became a steady glow. A car's air conditioner cycled on, almost drowning out his hiss. "Don't move. I think a car's driving through the lot."

Waiting for the thudding in her chest to fade, she closed her heavy eyelids and rested her forehead on his shoulder. "It's Officer Hensley and his new partner on patrol. Nine thirty-five every Saturday night."

"You *knew* somebody might catch us fooling around in your backseat?" He wiggled beneath her, like he was trying to make himself smaller.

Too sated to move, she let the night air cool her naked backside. "That's half the fun of it. Well, maybe a quarter. Gotta give sex the credit it deserves. You're not very adventurous, are you?"

"Why? Because I don't want to be arrested for public indecency?"

"Quit being melodramatic. They'll be gone in a minute."

"They're getting closer." His thigh spasmed against her calf and his palm closed over her left butt cheek.

She raised her head enough to roll her eyes at him, but it didn't distract her from the twitching half-hard dick inside her. "The only way they'll know we're here is if you keep fidgeting."

"I have a cramp in my foot."

Headlights swept across the upper third of the front seats and vanished as loose gravel crunched under the tires of the moving vehicle. Finally, the sounds faded, leaving only the occasional shoosh of a car on the main road and illumination from the security light.

She sat up, taking care to hold the used condom in place as she eased off Calloway's far-from-tiny-and-pathetic cock. A blind search of the dark floor yielded her cutoffs and underwear, but putting them on required more space than his body gave her. "Out, so I can get dressed."

After a struggle with his zipper and button, he stood on the seat and climbed out the passenger side. "Wait here a second. I have something for you."

Not flowers. She shoved her feet through the leg holes of her clothes and yanked them past her ass while he walked to his truck. By the time he returned, she'd settled into the driver's seat.

"Here." He handed her a legal-size envelope. "Read it when you get home."

Her gut warned her to hand it right back to him, but she tucked it under her purse and started Barry's engine. The calming purr covered her snort when he turned away without a goodnight, good-bye, or thank you, ma'am. He'd finally gotten the hint that she had no interest in his poor attempts at civility—pre- or post-copulation.

Exhaustion crept in on the drive home, and she yawned as she closed the garage door and carried the all-important envelope into the kitchen. Andria had left the light on over the sink, its warm glow casting illumination across the room. Still, the house held no welcoming presence. As much as Roma valued her privacy, she missed her sister's attempts at banal conversation every night.

She'll be home tomorrow.

After a hot shower, she slipped on a clean tank and pajama shorts and headed to the solarium with the envelope. The low hum of the ceiling fan and the soft rustle of leaves greeted her at the wide doorway. Instead of twisting the dimmer switch, she let the moonlight through the windows guide her to the center of her private sanctuary.

A wonderful chill from the ceramic tile cooled her tired feet as she weaved through the jungle, and the earthy scent of ferns, Chlorophytum, and more than a dozen other kinds of plants cleared her mind. At the hanging papasan chair, she lit the three largest candles on the table, appreciative of Andria's recent addition to the retreat. The chair swayed when she curled up in the bowl-shaped cushion and removed the must-read contents from Lucas's parting gift.

A cover letter topped the stack of papers, but she slipped it behind the last page for a look at what seemed to be legal documents. The next sheet was a copy of her lease agreement with Glenn Frasier. Several lines were highlighted in yellow.

"The terms are transferrable only to the extent that both parties

agree to uphold the obligations set forth in this contract until expiration of the lease."

The other featured excerpt blurred as her temper exploded, but enough words came into focus to confirm that the following page was an official eviction announcement from his lawyer.

"You underhanded, scum-sucking worm." She flipped to the cover letter, all the calm generated from two orgasms, a shower, and her sanctuary gone. The polite tone of his notice to vacate the premises in thirty days set her blood boiling. Arrogance would soon be the least of Calloway's flaws. "Cutting off your balls and feeding them to the pigs is too good for you!"

A deep blast from her lungs extinguished the trio of candles in a single blow, and she stalked out of the solarium before it became contaminated by her anger. Every living thing in the room had perished during her only previous fatal infection—her first night home after Andria's rape. Destroying her sanctum hadn't changed a fucking thing.

She expelled the thought and renewed her wrath toward tonight's miscreant at the threshold to the living room. "You're going to pay for this."

The file cabinet in the corner of her home office offered retaliation, revenge, and reclamation. She pulled open the top drawer and thumbed through the alphabetical tabs until she reached the "L"s and then Lease. With a gratifying stab, she marked the spot with her letter knife and slid the file from its slot. Purpose transformed her rage from iron-smelting heat to a manageable simmer as she fired up the copy machine and made duplicates of the documents her landlord had neglected to include in his unenforceable claim.

Copies at the ready, she retrieved her cell from its charging cord in her bedroom and returned to sit at her desk. A search of her contacts was the next step in putting Lucas Calloway in his place. She tapped on her lawyer's number and waited through four rings.

"Hi, Roma." A noisy yawn followed his greeting. "Sorry. Excuse me. Is everything okay?"

She drummed her fingertips on the stack of fresh copies. "I need your legal assistance, Ben."

"What happened?" The sleep vanished from his voice. "Am I your one phone call? Do you need me to contact a bondsman? Which jail are you at? Medina County? I can be there in…half an hour."

A snicker and then an uncontrolled fit of giggles burst out of her. Leave it to her lawyer to assume the worst. Did he really think she'd assaulted someone? Or disturbed the peace?

"Talk to me, Roma. You only have a limited call time. Are you okay?"

She gasped through the laughter and swiped at the wetness on her cheeks. "I'm not… God, I'm much better now. Not in jail. I need you to send a cease-and-desist order. My new landlord is a jackass."

"Uh-oh. What did he do? Oh, and I'm glad you weren't arrested."

"It's still a possibility. He's trying to break the lease. Tonight he hand-delivered a notice to vacate the building."

"Didn't he get all the paperwork from Glenn? The lease agreement is binding until you break it."

"I know that and you know that, but Mr. Calloway threatened to have me bodily removed if I'm not out thirty days from now."

A feminine groan carried through the line. "Are the boys okay, Ben?"

"They're…um…fine." His embarrassment couldn't have been more apparent if he'd been standing in front of Roma with a beet-red face.

Roma leaned back in the chair and chuckled. "Benny, I didn't think you had it in you. The redhead?"

"No comment. What do you want me to do?"

Prepared for her greatest collaboration, she rubbed her hands together. "Here's the plan."

CHAPTER 6

The house hadn't changed much in eight years, and neither did Lucas's impulse to keep on driving when he reached the mailbox. If not for the promise he'd made to his mom, he would have.

Sunday dinner. Then he could cut out and spend the rest of the day working to shorten his visit to Wadsworth. The invitation to stay remained unspoken, but he wasn't delusional. The hints had been flying since he'd arrived six days ago. The direct questions weren't far off.

Surrendering to the unavoidable, he parked under the old oak several car lengths from the garage and set his phone to alert him at one thirty. Before he could pocket his cell, it rang in his hand. The number on the screen brought a mix of relief and concern. "Lucas Calloway. Hi, Andria. How are you?"

"Hi, Lucas. I'm well, thank you. I hope you're enjoying your weekend."

It's been interesting. "Yes."

"I've made a decision." Her follow-up silence lasted almost long enough to make him check the connection. "I'm accepting your offer."

Everything's falling into place. "I'm available this afternoon if you want to go ahead and take care of the tax and benefits forms. I can be at the center by one forty-five."

"Today?"

He leaned against the front fender, willing to put off his arrival in favor of convincing the new director to make his exit happen sooner. "I'm hoping you can start tomorrow morning. The sooner you're heading up the project, the sooner we can open the center."

"That makes sense. One forty-five is fine. Then I can stop in the gelato shop and let my sister know I'm back when we're finished."

"Sister?" The two women couldn't be more different in temperament or looks. *And interesting just got complicated.*

"Roma? I figured you knew she's my older sister, especially after you told me how easy it was to find my resume online. Although I should probably thank you for not digging into my family life."

"It wasn't relevant. I prefer to stay out of employees' personal business unless they have a criminal record."

"Sounds like a good policy. Things aren't always what they seem on the surface." Something in her voice said her past might possess an instance or two that fell into that category. "I have to go, but I'll see you in a couple hours."

"Okay. See you then." He rubbed at his furry jaw as he ended the call, unsure why he'd forgone shaving the entire previous week. He was overdue for a haircut too.

"Lucas." Affection colored his father's one-word greeting, the same way it had the numerous times he'd shown up in the principal's office to bail Lucas out of detention and suspension for fighting. Not once had he raised his voice or his hand to the kid who wouldn't stay out of trouble. The seventy-year-old version was a lot grayer, but his purposeful gait and welcoming smile were the same.

"Dad." Lucas stuffed his phone in his pocket as he pushed away from the truck. *Okay, so maybe I want to stay. But I can't.*

The usual handshake became the usual hug, the one thing he hoped would never change.

"I hope you're hungry. Your mom's grilling." Standing eye-to-eye with him, his father grinned. "I made triple-fudge brownies for dessert and bought a pint of Roma's stracciatella gelato for on top."

"Celebrating something?" Lucas fell into step beside his dad.

"Family." At the front porch, Brad Calloway put his arm around Lucas's shoulders. "My son is home."

My son. Those two words together had saved Lucas during his rough late elementary and middle school years. They'd also been the catalyst for every punch he'd thrown. By high school, the assholes had learned to keep their mouths shut about who his real father was—a dead rapist.

His mom met them at the door, an oven mitt on her left hand and tongs in her right, but that didn't stop her from kissing his cheek and hugging him. Her embrace lasted longer than the hugs she'd given him at the Foundation offices each time he'd seen her over the last six days. "I'm so glad you could make it."

When he caught the subtle blend of apricots and vanilla, he eased away. Thirty years after he'd given her perfume for Mother's Day, she still wore the scent. "Me too."

"Would you like something to drink? Water? Iced tea or coffee?" She hurried into the kitchen and to the cupboard by the sink. "Dinner will be ready in about twenty minutes."

"Water's fine, but I can get it." At her nod, he opened the cabinet that had contained an assortment of cups and glasses for as long as he could remember. *Time for a new topic.* "Andria accepted the position. I'm meeting with her this afternoon to make sure everything's ready for her to start tomorrow."

"That's terrific! I'm sure she'll do a wonderful job heading up the recovery center." His mom removed a casserole dish from the fridge and set it on the counter. "I appreciate your help with the project. With the fundraiser coming up next month, the staff and I have been incredibly busy."

His redirection led the conversation through the next two hours, providing a much more acceptable alternative to what likely would have been awkward silences and tense exchanges. He'd also managed to avoid the questions he didn't want to answer, at least until another day.

When he pulled into a diagonal parking space a block and a half up the street from his rental properties, Andria waved at him from the sidewalk. Her dog glanced his direction as he approached them, but Maxine seemed more watchful of the couple leaving the gelato shop. Two young boys popped out of the door after them.

Looks like the redhead snagged herself a prospective husband.

Andria met him at the curb. "They make a striking pair, don't they?"

Shaking her outstretched hand, he shrugged. "I guess so, but do they like each other or are they just desperate for a relationship?"

Her belly laugh drew the attention of another group exiting the storefront. More unsettling was the fact that the uninhibited amusement brought an unbidden image of a certain outspoken banshee to mind. Maybe the sisters were more alike than he'd initially thought, even though they shared few physical similarities.

Andria set off at a relaxed pace, her companion glued to her side. "You sound like Roma. I didn't think anyone could be as cynical about love as she is."

"I prefer to call it realistic. I don't need anyone to *complete* me. I'm as whole as I'll ever be." He inserted the key in the deadbolt and used the magic spell to unlock the door. "After you."

Entering ahead of him, she looked over her shoulder. "It's nice to have someone you can depend on for support. Somebody who understands and accepts you."

"I get that some people want that. Hell, my parents have been married for almost fifty years. But I'm pretty good at taking care of myself and I like it that way." He retrieved the file the Foundation's HR person had supplied and gestured for his guest to sit in one of the two chairs he'd added since his escapade with Roma on Friday. Keeping a copy for himself, he handed Andria the top set of papers. "You'll need to sign the contract first. It outlines your salary, health insurance, and other benefits. The second page talks about privacy policy, for your personal information and that of other employees and clients. It's identical to the one I included in the proposal, but you're welcome to read through it before you sign."

She reviewed every document and asked for clarification in all the places he would have, affirming he'd chosen the best candidate for the job. Maxine raised her head from her front paws as Andria inched forward on the chair with the last form. "You should know I almost declined your offer. Matt—my husband—and I spent most of the weekend talking about the pros and cons. Although it'll be difficult to deal directly with recent victims, we decided that this is an opportunity to make a big difference. I've given clothing, personal items, and money to help other survivors like me, but I can do more."

"I hope you find the job rewarding. The Foundation is thrilled to have you on the team." He rose from the seat beside her and straightened the stack of papers on the desk. "Not to overwhelm you, but I want you to think about how to best utilize the space upstairs so we can get started on the floor plan tomorrow. I have a construction crew lined up, just in case. You're welcome to look around again if you want to."

"Thanks. I'll let you know when I'm leaving."

He nodded as he carried the paperwork to the scanner he'd set up on a table against the wall. "Oh, and the office next door is yours. The furniture was delivered yesterday. The computer and printer are scheduled for tomorrow by ten."

The kid-in-a-candy-shop grin she aimed at him on her way out of the conference room matched her sister's. "Okay. Thanks."

Get out of my head, woman. More than likely, Roma Denata wouldn't be receptive to any more sex-capades after reading the contents of last night's post-coital envelope. He'd already exceeded the maximum number of fucks he gave to one female anyway. Another would only invite trouble.

Most of an hour passed before Andria reappeared in the doorway. "The floor plan is fine. I want to use the second-floor rooms for meditation, exercise classes, and yoga, besides larger group therapy sessions. The only problem is accessibility. With the money we're saving on renovations, I'm thinking we could look into installing an elevator or a chair lift in the stairway."

Enthusiasm. His instincts had been right on the money. "See what you can find out online about local installers and prices, and I'll make some phone calls tomorrow."

"Don't we have to submit a request to the Foundation? I'm sure there's a budget we have to adhere to."

He closed his laptop and leaned back in the desk chair. "There is, but I set the budget for improvements since I own the building. That includes all structural changes, plumbing, electrical, the security system, and whatever else to prepare the space for the center."

"So you're donating thousands of dollars of your own money to create the ideal space?" She studied him like she could see into his soul. "You're probably charging a dollar or something ridiculous for rent too."

Heat crept along his neck, but he refused to break eye contact first. "It's an investment, not to mention a tax deduction. You can ask to see the projected budget if you want to know the rent expense."

Her expression said she didn't believe his story. "I'll do that. In the meantime, I promise not to tell anyone how generous you are since it's purely speculation. See you bright and early tomorrow morning."

Maxine glanced back at him with a doggie grin as Andria turned toward the reception area. Even she seemed to think his excuses were a load of bullshit.

"I'll be here by eight." He flipped open his laptop and logged back in.

The numbers blurred in the spreadsheet, his attention no longer focused on the report his accountant had emailed last week. All that mattered was he had plenty of capital to fund the improvements, pay for the furniture, and provide the office equipment Andria and her staff would need to launch the Foundation's newest contribution.

Then I can get the hell out of town.

He spun to face the wall behind him and clear his mind. As he relaxed into the chair, Roma invaded his thoughts again. If anybody had told him he would get laid in the backseat of a car at thirty-eight years old, he would have laughed his ass off. The very real risk of being caught by the police had obviously been a huge turn-on for the sharp-tongued Italian wench too. He'd never been much of a wham-bam sex kind of guy, but she pushed him to the edge with that hot body and hotter temper. How pissed off was she at him for ending her lease? Enough to angry fuck him one more time?

Scrubbing his hands through his hair, he sighed. "Nothing fixes your problems like a good fuck."

"I agree." Her sultry tone whispered across his skin.

"What brings you here, Roma?" He nudged his chair around, prepared for a battle. Instead, his dick swelled to life for the naked beauty lounging crossways in the armchair on the opposite side of his desk. "Sex won't change my mind about the lease."

She swung her bare feet to the floor and stood in a single graceful motion. "I'm not interested in changing your mind about the lease. I want fucked."

Fire spread through him as she closed the distance between them. Wisps of dark curly hair caressed her shoulders, escapees from the messy knot atop her head, and her breasts swayed in time with her hips. She placed a hand on either arm of his chair and leaned close enough that he could suck a nipple into his mouth.

Then she straddled his lap and nibbled his ear. "Are you going to fuck me, Lucas?"

With her pussy inches from his straining dick, how could he deny her? Or himself?

"Yes." He scooped his palms under her ass and pushed upward. Her taut muscles and silky skin invited him to explore. "My turn to choose the position."

She tugged his shirt from the back of his shorts as he straightened. "Against the wall?"

"Nope. Put your feet down." Lowering her to the floor, he found her lips and traced them with his tongue. A dip inside proved hard to resist, and he gave in without a fight.

She welcomed him, gliding her tongue along his in a slow dance instead of a skirmish. The slow, easy rhythm seduced him as fast as their punishing kisses, but it invited him to take her to bed for a whole night of lovemaking—which would cross one of the boundaries he'd set for himself long ago.

Breaking the kiss, he turned her in his arms and bent her over the desk. "I want to fuck you from behind."

She wiggled her ass at him, tempting him to skip suiting up.

No condom, no sex. After a quick zip, tear, and roll, he guided his erection through her slick folds until she arched against him and he slipped inside her. The squeeze and release of her pussy promised him heaven, sooner than later. The curve of her ass against his lower belly practically guaranteed it.

"Mmm. I can feel you so deep. Fuck me. Hard and fast."

Consumed by her demand, he cupped her breast in one hand and found her clit with the other. He rocked into her, flicking her taut nipple and stroking her swollen bud to accommodate her request. Every thrust brought a rush of tightness to his balls, stealing more of his control, but her endless gasps and groans persuaded him that wasn't a bad thing.

A piercing cry accompanied the sudden grip and release of his cock in her body, sending him hurtling into a weightless world of utter bliss. Heat shot up his dick and he let the orgasm carry him away with her.

He collapsed on top of her, too caught up in the erratic aftershocks emanating from her body to do more than hope their breathing returned to normal at some point. Her hair tickled his chin, but he didn't move away. Holding her soothed the most damaged part of him, even if it was temporary.

"Get off me. I have to get back to work." The connection abruptly ended when she pushed him away.

Once again, his sheathed dick lay half limp outside his zipper. Maybe Roma had wham-bammed him instead of the other way around. For the fourth time in as many days, they'd banged each other senseless and gone about their business as if nothing had happened.

Still naked, she slid a large envelope toward him on the desk and then sauntered across the room. Partway out the door, she winked at him over her bare shoulder. "Read it *before* you go home."

CHAPTER 7

"You okay?"

Roma lifted her head from her arm pillow, not sure how much time had passed since she'd yanked on her clothes and returned to the gelato shop. "Yeah. Just hit a wall. How long was I out?"

"Almost half an hour." Tess scrunched her nose and frowned. "Your cheeks are flushed and your eyes are glassy. Should I see if Addie or Gwen can work until close?"

A monumental orgasm and the supreme satisfaction of exacting revenge will do that to you. "Nah. I'm fine. I'll be out in a sec."

"Okay." After another penetrating stare, her employee finally disappeared into the kitchen.

I wonder if Mr. Landlord knows he's stuck with me yet. The knowledge that Calloway was probably scrambling in his wingtips for a nonexistent loophole rejuvenated Roma as much as the post-sex nap.

She stretched as she stood, confident she could easily smack the smugness off Lucas's face with a cup of lemon gelato if he ever called her short stuff again. While she didn't like wasting her tasty creations, it would fit his sour disposition perfectly.

The smell of fresh waffle cones lured her to the service counter. A horde of noisy miniature soccer players crowded through the entrance as she washed and dried her hands. "Who won today?"

The tallest of the under-ten mob smirked at her from beyond the step-up shelf. He was usually the loudest and the first to brag about his exploits on the field. "We did. I'd like a—"

"Hold on." She wielded a scoop and smirked right back at him. "Swing the end of the line over here to the counter. I'm playing my reverse card today. And quiet earns you an extra scoop of vanilla or chocolate."

A raucous cheer echoed off the walls and then silenced almost as quickly as the kids lined up through the tables curved around to the freezer case.

"That's not fair. You're our sponsor." The boy at the former head of the line frowned and crossed his arms at his chest.

"My mood, my rules. It's not like I'm going to run out even if you all order the same flavor. Besides, we already won the game. No need to be jerks by rubbing their noses in it."

He shrugged and sighed, clearly not happy with her reasoning.

Less than ten minutes later, she handed him a waffle bowl with two scoops of chocolate. "Told ya I had enough. Good job waiting your turn."

"Thanks, I guess."

"You're welcome, I guess." She shared an eye roll with his coach at the grudging thanks before a scene on the sidewalk grabbed her interest.

Glenn Frasier stood with his back partway to her in a pair of checked shorts and an orange golf shirt. Her nemesis wore the same bad-boy attitude he'd had on since the day she'd first crossed paths with him. The older man appeared to laugh at something his nephew said and Lucas jabbed his finger toward the shop.

"Ooh, somebody looks ticked off." Tess's observation was likely an understatement. "It wouldn't have anything to do with that envelope you took next door earlier, would it?"

"I hope so." Roma met her adversary's glare through the window and waved. *Serves you right for being an ass.* "That was my intent after all."

He stormed toward the door, but Glenn caught him by the elbow. More pointing and one-sided discussion ensued before the old man dragged his nephew out of sight.

Good riddance to egotistical trash.

"Here's the register tape from the soccer invasion." Tess chuckled as she leaned in. "He's the guy, isn't he? Definite biker vibe and kinda hot for not being my type."

Taking the receipt, Roma snorted. "I'll be sure to tell him. And you know I don't fuck and tell."

"You don't need to tell. There's enough steam coming off you to melt the polar ice caps, but your secret's safe with me." A shoulder bump and giggle said her employee found it too funny not to share with her live-in girlfriend. "If you'll bring out new pans of vanilla bean, chocolate, and dulce de leche, I'll pull the empty ones and restock cups and spoons."

Glad for the mindless distraction, Roma nodded and set off for the kitchen. Out of sight didn't necessarily mean out of mind, but a few minutes with her head in the freezer might shrink the memory of today's not-compensating dick.

Luckily, her neighbor stayed on his own side of the wall the remainder of the day. His truck sat three parking spaces up from Barry in the rear lot again, but neither hide nor hair of him showed up when she locked up for the night. Perspiration from her Sunday night deep clean had soaked her tank top, and the balmy air cooled her skin, if not her wandering mind.

You can read that addendum forward, backward, and upside down. There's no way in hell you're breaking my lease.

She gunned the engine to celebrate as she pulled out of the lot, making the tires squeal on the still-warm pavement. Blue and red lights flashed behind her on the side street half a second later. Stopping in the middle of the lane, she shifted into neutral and engaged the emergency brake. *Damn it, Hensley. I just want to go home and take a shower.*

The officer moseyed toward her car, his badge and dentist-whitened smile glinting in her side mirror. "Evening, Roma."

"Tom. Blacktop's really holding the heat tonight, isn't it?" She handed him her driver's license and registration.

He waved them away. "We both know your lead foot and hot temper are responsible. That's not why I stopped you, though. Word is there's been a rash of stolen cars in the area. Classics and old muscle cars like yours. The 'Cuda is an easy mark, especially with its top down. You might consider leaving it in the garage until the perpetrators are caught."

"Thanks for the heads-up. Anything else?" She tapped her thumb on the steering wheel.

His grimace didn't bode well for a quick escape. "I thought I saw somebody hanging around your car last night before you left. We drove through, but whoever it was must've seen us coming and run off. Be careful when you're leaving, okay? You never know what some people will do for a fast buck."

The inside of her lip hurt like a son of a bitch from biting it, but giving herself away was not an option. "Will do. If there's nothing else, I need to get going."

"Have a good night." He gave a curt nod and walked back toward the squad car.

No more sex in the parking lot. She returned her license and registration to their rightful places and headed for home.

The setting sun reflected off the living room and solarium windows as she turned into the driveway and pressed the garage door button on her visor. Andria's staid sedan sat in the right half, bringing relief and consternation. Earlier, she'd deflected Roma's innocuous questions about her trip and skipped out after only an "I'm back" greeting and a "Have to unpack and do laundry" farewell.

Something's going on.

With her purse slung over her shoulder, Roma closed the garage door and let herself into the kitchen. Muted conversation came from the living room, but *Nonna*'s no-nonsense cadence was unmistakable. "Anybody home?"

"You're early." Her sister blinked and glanced toward their grandmother as Roma entered the room. Maxine made eye contact, but she didn't raise her head.

"The last half hour was a little slower than average, so Tess and I got a head start on cleanup." Roma crossed to the rocking chair and leaned down to kiss her grandma's wrinkly cheek. "Hi, *Nonna*. What brings you here? Do you need a ride home?"

"What?" *Nonna* tsked and cast a furtive look in Andria's direction. "I can't visit my *nipotina* when I want? And you want me to leave? I stay as long as I like."

The sense of secrecy spiked, sending Roma down the hall. "I'm going to take a shower. You're welcome to sleep in my bed if you spend the night. I have work to do anyway."

Low voices followed her as she walked into the bathroom, but shutting the door locked them out. She dragged her tank top and bra over her head and kicked off her shorts and underwear. Steam billowed past the shower curtain, collecting on the mirror and blurring her naked reflection long before she stepped under the scalding spray.

I hate secrets.

People hid behind false impressions and they deceived those around them with subversive tidbits of information. She'd had no secrets, but the world hadn't given a damn when she'd been trapped in the spotlight. Her whole life had been scrutinized because of one secret—a secret that hadn't even been her own.

A knock made her heart rate jump and stutter.

"Roma, I'm taking *Nonna* home. I'll be back in fifteen minutes."

She grunted her acknowledgment rather than risking an uncensored response.

"And can you wait to work on last week's bookkeeping? I need to talk to you about something important."

What now? "Sure."

"Thanks. See you shortly."

A million scenarios flitted through Roma's mind, adding to her irritability. The doctor had said Andria was in excellent health at her checkup last month. Her car had had an oil change and maintenance check before her weekend trip. Maxine's visit to the vet had been perfect. Was some prick stalking them?

With no chance of relaxation from the pelting jets, she shut off the faucet and buried her face in the thick towel hanging over the shower rod. Most of her thoughts were impossibly ridiculous and undeserving of the tension they inspired, but the prospect of a stalker or some other predator sent chills down her spine.

Breathe. It's probably nothing.

Refocusing her thoughts on the shop's income report, she rubbed her skin dry, wrapped the towel around her wet hair, and traipsed to her bedroom for pajamas. Andria would be home any minute and Roma would solve whatever issue needed taken care of, including the removal of any predatory males from their lives. That was her role in their world.

Her curls mostly under control and her determination back in place, Roma padded to the fridge in search of supper. A foil container with her name on it and a see-through plastic bowl filled with lettuce and a handful of grape tomatoes occupied the official leftovers shelf.

What the hell?

Beggars couldn't be choosers, not that she was a picky eater. She had, however, become accustomed to Andria's home-cooked meals during the four years they'd lived together. Her sister vilified most restaurant food on a regular basis, claiming she could cook a hundred times better—and rightly so. Why on earth would she bring carryout into the house?

The low hum of the garage door opener announced her return as Roma dumped the generous portion of bacon-laced mac and cheese on a paper plate. After a thorough scrape of the aluminum pan, she put her entrée in the microwave and pried the lid off the salad. Halfway through the reheat cycle, Andria and Maxine strolled past the breakfast nook window, both seemingly engrossed in their evening walk.

Something's wrong. I can feel it.

With her dinner and a glass of milk on the table, Roma sat facing the entrance her sister always used. Sunset faded to dusk before the door clicked open. She set her fork on the plate mid bite and pushed out the chair adjacent to her with her bare foot. "What's going on?"

Andria crossed to the table with Maxine shadowing her, but she didn't sit. Her fingers closed over the arched back of the chair. "It's nothing bad. I'm just changing jobs."

"But you like working from home and setting your own hours. You've been damn successful at the freelancing gig." *And you're safer here.*

"I'm ready to try something new." Gesturing for her companion to lie down, Andria paced to the stove and back. "It's an amazing opportunity and I can put my organizational skills to better use. The pay is decent. I have good benefits. Plus, I'll be closer to you."

Roma's stomach rumbled for its dinner, but she ignored it. "What's the position? Where will you be working? You can take Maxine to work with you, can't you?"

"Maxine is welcome. It was the first question I asked." Her sister pulled a trifold pamphlet from her purse and set it on the table. "I'll be organizing and managing a new rape recovery and resource center next to the gelato shop. This is a mock-up of the information we'll be distributing. Look at the types of services we're hoping to provide. I start tomorrow."

Her appetite shriveling to nothing, Roma pushed aside her plate and grabbed the pamphlet. "Are you sure you want to do this? I mean, you'll have to… Day after day."

"I have the opportunity to help people. How is that a bad thing?"

The location leapt off the page, its lettering in large bold font beneath the name of the center. "Look at this! Every pervert on the planet is going to know where to find you."

Andria yanked the paper from Roma's hands, the creases radiating from her frown a fair indication that she was digging her heels in. "No, every rape victim will know where to find us. Not everybody wants to report it. Ah, hell. Who are we kidding? *Most* of us don't report, and those people can't get help if they don't know services are available. Hiding only perpetuates the stigma. We're not the bad guys and we didn't do anything wrong."

"Fine, you're not wrong about that, but how are you going to stop the SOBs who want to keep their victims quiet from coming in and shooting up the place and everybody in it?" The pulse drumming in Roma's chest moved to her head. "Do you really believe anybody who's scared to death of reporting is going to feel safe there?"

"Lucas and I talked about security. He—"

"*Lucas*? As in Lucas Calloway?" Roma shoved her chair back, toppling it behind her as she stood. "What the hell does that lowlife prickster have to do with this?"

Andria's chin dropped, the realization of her mistake evidently dawning. "What a horrible thing to say about someone you don't even know."

"I know him well enough. Did he tell you he tried reneging on the lease I had with Glenn?"

"Why would he do that? He's working with the Calloway Foundation to start up the center next door to you."

You're too damn naïve to see the truth. "Ha! I bet he's charging them an arm and a leg to rent the building too. Would you like to read the get-the-hell-out-of-your-space-in-thirty-days letter he gave me yesterday? I'm sure you'd be quite enlightened about his underhanded business tactics."

The color drained from Andria's face. "He didn't tell me he was terminating your lease."

"Did you expect him to? At least I had the foresight to insist on some additions to the terms when the original lease came up for renewal the first time. That bastard can't kick me out unless I decide to leave. You might want to submit your resignation now."

CHAPTER 8

"What do you mean there's nothing you can do? Her five-year lease expires next month." Lucas held the phone against his ear with his shoulder, balanced his first cup of coffee of the morning in his left hand, and shoved his key in the lock with his right. A jiggle and a nudge became a jerk and a kick, but the only things that budged were the strap of his computer bag from his left shoulder to his elbow and a geyser of coffee onto his shoe. *I hate these fucking locks.*

"Doesn't matter. It's ironclad. She either knew exactly how to tie this lease down forever or hired somebody who did." His attorney chuckled, adding to Lucas's annoyance. "I gotta say I'm impressed by her ingenuity."

"That's not the answer I wanted to hear." Giving up on the front entrance, Lucas trudged to the alley leading to the back of the building.

"Look, unless you want to file a failure-to-disclose complaint against Glenn and nullify your purchase contract, you're without a case. You have no choice but to honor the prior lease terms, including addendums he may or may not have shared with you. State law. Even if he didn't understand what he was signing, it's still binding—to both of you and any future owners. Automatic renewal until she terminates the lease. It's that simple. At least she didn't insist on no rent increases in perpetuity."

At the rear entrance, he stabbed the key into the lock and twisted. "I don't give a damn about the money. I want the space. She's between two properties that are going to house Foundation projects."

"I suggest you find someplace else for whatever you have planned, because she has the legal right to be there for as long as she wants. Just pulled into the parking garage. I'll talk to you later. Good luck."

"Luck has nothing to do with it." *Except when I'm trying to open the goddamn front door.* He ended the call and shoved his phone in his pants pocket before tackling the heavy-duty doorknob. As the door swung open, movement to his right drew his attention.

Roma, wearing her signature cutoffs and tank top, bent to pick up something from the ground less than fifteen feet away. The view of her shapely ass triggered the memory of yesterday's desk fuck and a twitch in his dick. She looked his direction, but she didn't wave or taunt him. Her menacing stare threatened him with bodily harm if he dared approach her for a daily helping of fast-and-furious sex.

What does she have to be pissed off about?

He stepped inside and closed the door before he did something more foolish than Uncle Glenn had done—like run next door for an early-morning fuck. She'd bested him in the landlord-tenant battle, but the attraction didn't have to end in his humiliation. Her intelligence and creative thinking skills made him want to explore more than her body. She was his equal, in business and sexual prowess.

Smart, sexy, and a challenging adversary. If she'd acted like she had any interest in a relationship, he never would have been tempted to abandon his long-held conviction to keep his distance.

Temptation doesn't require follow through.

He dropped off his coffee and computer bag at his desk and headed for the restroom to clean his shoe. His return to the reception area a few minutes later only aggravated his already cranky disposition. If the front door wouldn't unlock from the inside, he'd rip the stupid thing off its hinges.

Andria stood on the other side, looking almost as livid as her sister.

Just what I need—another angry female.

When a tug on the handle didn't achieve anything, she wielded the key he'd given her yesterday and worked her locksmith's-daughter magic before he could let her and her guard dog in. "Your office. Now. We need to talk."

He nodded and trailed after her to the room he'd claimed. "Is there a problem?"

"You could say that." Instead of sitting, she plopped her tote bag on the chair and withdrew a folder. Her palm smacked the surface of the desk as she set a typed document down in front of him. "Explain this. And you better tell the truth or I'm submitting my resignation, effective immediately."

Pretty sure she would quit anyway if she didn't like his explanation, he picked up what seemed to be some sort of correspondence. *"Dear Ms. Denata, This is to inform you that your lease will not be renewed upon the anniversary date of the original agreement."*

"Did you write this letter?"

He rounded the desk and retrieved the envelope Roma had delivered after their impromptu tryst from the top file-cabinet drawer. A copy of the entire contents of his envelope rested in the file directly behind hers, but he left it where it was and sat. "Yes, I wrote it. Have you seen her response?"

Andria's left eyebrow rose half an inch and she looked down her nose at him. "No, but I would imagine she used every swear word known to man to tell you what she thinks of you. To be honest, I'm inclined to agree with her. She's been at this location since she started her business fifteen years ago, and giving her a month's notice to vacate the premises is reprehensible. I got the impression you're a shrewd businessman when you contacted me about the interview, but this... This is about as Scrooge-y as a person can get. Ruthless, greedy, and unfeeling. I'm incredibly disappointed in you."

"Her response." He handed her the packet of documents and steepled his fingers under his chin as he leaned back. "After you read it, I'll explain my motivation."

Several minutes passed while she shuffled through the pages, pausing to likely skim the contents of each one. A wicked smile identical to her sister's grew with every sheet. "*Mio Dio*, I had no idea she negotiated these terms. I knew she was smart, but this is pure genius."

"My lawyer thought so too."

She straightened the stack of papers against the desk and returned his comeuppance to the envelope. "What about you?"

A resigned laugh escaped. "Let's just say I wish she hadn't thought of it, especially since it's thrown a permanent wrench into my plans. I'm still fuming at Glenn for not telling me about the addendum, but I suppose I can't blame Roma for his lack of foresight."

"Maybe he *wanted* her to have a perpetual lease, in case something happened to him. Glenn's always had a soft spot for my sister." Andria finally settled into the chair with Maxine at her feet.

Combing his hands through his hair, he snorted. "He called her sweet when he told me about her. I think we both know that's a significant exaggeration."

"Maybe, but she's the most loyal person I've ever known." The softness of the words suggested Andria had been a long-time recipient of that loyalty. "Why do you want her storefront?"

His laptop contained the notes he'd made during the conference call that had initiated the project. However, he didn't need to look at them to remember the idea he'd tossed onto the table and the Board had unanimously approved. It was the single element he'd truly looked forward to spearheading. "The plan was to open a self-sustaining small business managed and run by clients from the center to help them get out of abusive relationships. Intimate-partner rape statistics are around thirty percent and reporting doesn't do any good if the victim has no way of supporting herself if she leaves."

"You're a Type A personality, aren't you?" The question sounded like an accusation.

"I like being a Type A. I'm most comfortable when I'm in charge."

"Is there a particular reason you didn't ask Roma about hiring clients in those situations? She has a well-established business that's financially stable. During the busiest season, she has a minimum of three part-time employees. They're typically college students, but she might be willing to change that aspect of her business plan. She's also female and understands what these women have experienced. Why do you need to start from scratch?"

A lone embarrassing excuse rang true in his head. He shrugged and sighed. "I didn't consider it because I didn't think of it. People like me tend to do everything themselves so it's done right."

"Yes, I know. My sister is like that. For that admission, I'll withdraw my pending resignation. Would you like me to set up a meeting with Roma to discuss your idea?" Andria edged forward in the chair, her hands clasped on her lap. "An apology might smooth the road. It depends on how much you want to do this."

I want to do Roma across that chair. "If you can convince her to talk to me, I'll apologize, even though the lease issue wasn't personal."

"And if you sound half as insincere to her as you do to me, she'll tell you where to stick your apology. She might even stick it there for you."

He fought a chuckle and lost. "I have no doubt she would. I promise to do better."

With a nod, she removed her cell from the tote. "When and where can you meet?"

"Whatever's convenient for her." *Now. Anywhere we can get naked.*

"Okay. I'll let you know when I hear back from her." Andria tapped on the screen as she stood. "It may take a little arm-twisting to talk her into this, so you should probably find us both something to do until my computer arrives."

Properly put in his place by the younger Denata sister, he retrieved his laptop and powered it on. "I have a list. I'll meet you in your office in five minutes."

Maxine accompanied her out of the room after a look that included a doggie smile and a wag of her tail.

Yes, I know I'm not in charge anymore. You don't have to rub it in.

Concentrating on distractions from the memories that had given him a hard-on, he emailed his to-do list to the new director and sent a text message to the contractor he'd lined up for renovations. After a phone call to the security technician, he carried his laptop to the office next to his and knocked on the doorjamb.

"Come in." Andria had donned a pair of glasses, giving her the all-business quality he'd found online during his pre-interview research. Her phone chimed as she pulled a picture frame from her bag. She carefully laid it glass-side up in the middle of the desk before picking up her phone, the picture obviously holding a special place in her heart. "That's probably Roma."

He sat in the visitor chair the furniture delivery guys had placed directly across from the director's workspace. The position allowed him a clear view of the photograph—a wedding picture of Andria and the man who had to be her ex-husband. Curiosity almost tricked him into asking how they'd found their way back to each other, but it was none of his business.

Her grimace told him all he needed to know about the text message. "She's not receptive to meeting at the moment. She was still mad at me this morning for taking the job without discussing it with her first. I'll talk to her at lunchtime. Maybe by then, her temper will have cooled off some."

"Did she swear at you too? Glenn and I got an earful of Italian the other day." He logged into his laptop in hopes of heading off the images of their clash in her kitchen before his uncle had arrived.

"I can't say that I blame her. From what I heard, you two weren't exactly upfront about the property changing hands. Besides, she's always angry about something." Andria brushed her fingers along the edge of the silver frame before standing it near the front corner of the desk. "There's never a good time to tell her something she doesn't want to hear. And, no, she doesn't swear at me. Ever."

"I think she saves it all for me." The document on the screen blurred as his mind wandered again.

"Her mechanic was on the receiving end last week. He let somebody drive her car without asking her first, not that she'd say yes. Barry's the closest thing she's had to a boyfriend in a long time."

"Barry? She's dating her mechanic?" The panic evident in his tone added to his bad mood.

Andria snickered. "Barry's her car. Short for Barracuda."

Relief replaced the unexpected feeling, but frustration remained. "Who names their car?"

"Interesting."

"What is?" He clicked on his calendar to count the days until he could leave town.

She was quiet for several moments, her expression suggesting she hadn't made up her mind whether or not to answer his question. "Just an observation, but you sounded jealous. Do you like my sister?"

Looking up at Andria, he grunted, hoping the cold sweat spreading across his shoulders and neck didn't show on his face. "She's easily the most spiteful and argumentative woman I've ever met."

The tilt of her head, a lopsided smirk, and raised eyebrows warned him she wasn't done with her interrogation. "But you like her anyway, don't you? And you're as freaked out by it as she would be. Probably is."

"I can practically guarantee she doesn't like me any more than I like her." He stopped himself from crossing his arms in front of his chest. "You should've seen the scowl she gave me this morning when I was trying to get in the building."

Andria's laughter filled the room. "You two are so much alike. Deny it all you want, but facts are facts. You've gotten under each other's skin and it's driving you crazy."

The cold sweat traveled over more of his torso, but the reminder that he'd touched her skin and been under, over, and inside her turned it hot.

"If it's any consolation, I bet she won't admit it, either."

You want an admission? I'll give you one. "I'm attracted to her. That doesn't mean I like her, and you probably don't want to know what it *does* mean."

A shrug accompanied a wave of her hand. "You and Roma are using each other for sex. Big deal. You're hardly the first, but Roma's usually much more discreet. She's been extremely moody the past several days, which tells me it's happened multiple times instead of the one-hit-wonder pattern she's followed in the past."

He closed his computer and stood, too unnerved by the speculation to sit still. "So the sex is better than average. We don't have to like each other to appreciate sexual chemistry."

"As I said, you can deny what you feel, but it doesn't change anything. Take it from someone who spent three and a half years in denial." Andria gestured toward the chair. "Sit. We have work to do."

Swallowing against the knot of panic in his throat, he surrendered to her instructions.

When did I lose control of my life?

CHAPTER 9

"Hey, boss, you got a minute?" Tess's tentative question came from the doorway leading to the service counter.

Roma sealed the bag and wielded her rolling pin, ready to vent her bad mood on the stacks of leftover waffle cones and bowls. "Depends on who needs what."

"Cliff's here. He wants to talk to you. He says it's important."

"He wouldn't know important if it chewed his dick off." Instead of using the rolling pin to crush the waffles into crumbs, Roma laid the bag on the worktable and whacked it with her fist. "I'm busy."

"You have to talk to Monte." Cliff's panicked voice tempted her to heave the wooden cylinder at him. "I need my job back. Angelica is…"

"Pressing charges for contributing to the delinquency of a minor?" She pounded the broken pieces again.

Cliff aimed a pleading look toward Tess until she shook her head and returned to the front of the store. "She says she's pregnant and I have to pay for doctor bills and child support. She's gonna have me arrested if I don't give her five hundred dollars by the end of the week."

"Jesus. I really overestimated your intelligence." After flipping over the bag, Roma switched to the rolling pin. The crunch and grind imparted much less satisfaction, but saving her hand in case she needed to punch him in the face seemed wise. "You fucked her last Wednesday night for the first time, am I right?"

"Yeah." Not a hint of comprehension dawned in his eyes.

"Cliff, it hasn't even been a week. She can't possibly know if she's pregnant. You used protection, didn't you?" *I've seen smarter ten-year-olds.*

"'Course I did. I'm not stupid."

I beg to differ. "Then you need to tell her you're taking her to Planned Parenthood for a pregnancy test before you're paying her a dime. If the test comes back positive, demand a paternity test. Based on her blackmail attempt, I'd guess she was already knocked up by somebody else before she suckered you into screwing her. Or she's pissed because you called her a mistake."

"Oh." The light finally came on in his eyes, dim as it was. "What if it's mine?"

"If it's your kid, man up. Be a responsible father. Marry the girl if you want to. Don't be a dickhead."

"Okay." He turned like he planned to leave, but he stopped. "Will you talk to Monte?"

She pointed the rolling pin at him. "Are you going to *borrow* a customer's car for a joyride ever again?"

"No." He shook his head. "I shouldn'ta let Angel talk me into it. I'm sorry."

Shit. I didn't think you'd apologize. "Are you going to get the hell out of my kitchen and leave me alone?"

His eyes widened as he nodded. "Yes, ma'am."

"Fine, I'll talk to him. Now get out so I can work."

He took half a step toward her, but then he changed direction and scurried through the doorway.

"You better run, you little toad." She mashed the remaining chunks of cone, wishing the task was a better outlet for her simmering prickliness. Why did so many people have to piss her off?

"Sorry to bother you again, but Andria's here." Tess peeked around the doorway, evidently aware that she might be taking her life in her hands if she entered the kitchen. "Do you have time to see her? She said it won't take long."

Why the hell can't everybody just let me seethe in peace? "Two minutes. And only if it doesn't have anything to do with her new employer." Satisfied with the size of the waffle crumbs, Roma emptied the bag into a plastic container and snapped on the lid.

"Lucas isn't my employer. The Calloway Foundation is." Andria walked past Tess into the kitchen, her frown promising no improvement over the last visitor. Her censuring look matched her conservative pantsuit, schoolmarm glasses, and uptight hairdo perfectly. "You didn't tell me you gave him a copy of the lease and the *addendum* that prevents him from kicking you out of the building."

"He tried to, which makes him a—"

"No name-calling please. Do you know why he wants you to vacate the building?"

"I don't give a damn why. I have a business to protect and I'm not leaving until I'm dead. And I plan to come back to haunt that slimy, underhanded piece of—"

"Roma." Her sister channeled their mother's admonishing tone she'd used often during Roma's teenage years. "He's sorry for…the absence of tact."

"Lucas Calloway? Sorry? Bullshit. The only thing he's sorry about is not being able to break the lease." Setting aside the container, Roma ticked down her mental to-do list. "And he wouldn't know tact if it bit him on the balls."

A twitch in Andria's jaw was the only acknowledgment of the insult. "Will you at least meet with him? He wants to apologize and ask you about an alternate idea. One that doesn't involve moving or closing the shop."

"Apologizing must not be particularly important to him, or he wouldn't have sent you. And if you know so much about the idea, why don't *you* give me the details?" Roma hurried into the walk-in cooler, glad for the rush of cool air on her bare arms and legs. With luck, it would ease the itch that had been eating at her since their near miss this morning at the rear entrance.

She hefted the bucket of vanilla-bean mix and returned to the worktable.

Andria still stood in the same spot. "Why do you dislike him so much?"

"You mean besides the fact that he's a misogynistic, egotistical jackass?" Ladle in hand, Roma scooped the mixture into the churn. "Let's see. He's rude. Underhanded—which I already mentioned. Dishonest. Sneaky. Shall I go on?"

"You see? That's exactly why he didn't come over here himself. You can't go ten seconds without insulting him."

"Only when he deserves it. Your two minutes are up. I have work to do." Roma hooked the ladle on the rim of the bucket and grabbed the container of waffle crumbs to dump in a generous helping. "Don't bother picking up supper for me tonight. I can feed myself."

"I was hoping we could eat together when you get home. Don't be like this, Roma."

"Like what? My usual bitchy self?" The lid clanked as she put it into place and locked it down, but a flip of the motor switch secured an end to the conversation with her sister. A surreptitious glance toward the front of the shop confirmed Andria had decided not to press the issue—at least for now. *The next person to interrupt my day better be fast on his feet because my give-a-shit-quotient is gone.*

The steady hum of the churn blocked out everything in the office but the occasional low *thunk* of the cash register closing while she prepared and submitted Tuesday's dairy order and compared the current month-to-date sales numbers to last year's. The background noise kept her mind focused on her work instead of a certain cock that needed to be detachable from its owner.

"Knock, knock." Tess's voice pulled Roma from the second to last item on her daily list before closing. "Got a second?"

Looking up from next week's schedule, she heaved a sigh. "Jesus Christ. No more visitors, and I don't want to hear about any problems. I trust you to handle the store."

The young woman leaned against the doorjamb and grinned. "Okay, then I'm calling in Addie or Gwen to work three to close today so you can have a night off. Go have supper with your *nonna* or something. You haven't had more than a half-hour break since we started summer hours in May."

"That's a hell of a lot more than a night. Besides, *Nonna* has euchre club tonight and I don't need a break."

"Really? Could've fooled me. I don't think I've ever seen you this grouchy the entire time I've worked here." Tess slipped her cell from the hidden pocket of her ruffled skirt. "Go pick up some spicy Mexican food and a hottie. You need to burn off that foul mood."

Adjusting the grip on her pen, Roma scowled. "Fine. I'll take a few hours off *if* one of the other girls is available, but I'm leaving at four instead of three—and no men. I don't need a guy for an orgasm. They're not worth the trouble."

"Wow, I expected more of an argument. I'm texting Addie now. If she's not free, I'll check with Gwen. If she can't work, I'm finding somebody off the street. One way or another, you're taking the rest of the day off." Tess tapped on the screen of her phone and disappeared into the kitchen faster than Roma could raise any objections.

"And people wonder why I'm cranky." Roma pushed away from her desk, ready to relieve her pushy part-timer.

"I heard that."

She followed Tess's admonishment toward the front of the shop. "Good."

"Addie says she can be here in twenty minutes. I'm running up the street for a veggie pita. I'll be back before it's time for you to leave. At three." With a perky wave, Tess rushed out the front door.

"Four, damn it." Growling at the empty—and spotless—tables, Roma assessed the supplies behind the counter and in the freezer case. Nothing needed done, not even a change of water for the scoop bucket. She found empty trashcans, a clean bathroom, and fingerprint-less glass across the windows facing the sidewalk. Even the step in front of the counter had been swept and mopped. Her most-senior employee hadn't left anything undone to use for an excuse to stay even an extra fifteen seconds, let alone until four or even three. "What the fuck am I going to do with an extra six hours?"

"You might try meditating or playing a video game where you can blows things up." Her lawyer chuckled behind her. "I saw Tess on my walk down the street. She told me she gave you the day off."

"Gave? Forced me is more like it." She marched to the server side of the counter and washed her hands. "Don't tell me. One scoop of vanilla in a cup."

Ben sauntered closer to the freezer case. "Actually, I was thinking of trying something new. How about half a scoop of dark chocolate and half a scoop of mint? Do you recommend the regular or chocolate waffle bowl with that?"

"Getting adventurous since you have a girlfriend?" She separated a bowl from the darker stack and lifted a scoop out of the bucket. "You know, missionary isn't the only sexual position."

His neck and cheeks flushed crimson, but a broad smile spread across his face. "Yes, I do know. Thanks for the matchmaking help. I owe you. Speaking of owing you, how did your landlord take the news?"

Using the same technique she employed for his son's split-scoop special, she released the bi-color sphere of gelato into the bowl. "He was adequately infuriated, made a scene with Glenn on the sidewalk, and, according to my sister, now wants to apologize for his absence of tact."

"So he wants something in return."

"Of course he does. Doesn't everybody?"

He set a stack of ones by the register and shrugged. "Not everybody. Keep the change."

"Lucas Calloway doesn't do anything without expecting some ROI. I know his type. I hope he chokes on his apology, because I have no use for it." A quick count of the cash revealed a gratuity greater than his bill. "Thanks for the tip. The girls will appreciate the extra income."

"You're welcome. I have to get back to the office, but let me know if you have any more lease issues." As Ben exited the shop, he held the door for Tess and then Addie. "See you tomorrow."

For a stodgy lawyer, he wasn't so bad, not that she'd ever view him as anything other than a boring but polite acquaintance.

"Hey, Roma." Addie hurried past the counter toward the kitchen. A few seconds later, she reappeared with an apron hanging around her neck and the strings dangling down her legs. "I appreciate the extra hours, especially after how much I'll have to spend on books next month."

Meeting Tess's amused gaze, Roma rolled her eyes. "I guess that's my cue to leave."

After a stop in her office to order a bbq-bacon-and-cheddar burger from the café and grab her purse, she headed out for her involuntary break. The drive to Silver Creek Park gave her ten minutes to savor the mouthwatering aroma of her early supper and work up an appetite. Although the trailhead lot closest to the lake wasn't parked full, she continued to the paved parking area between the hiking trails to avoid the summer crowd near the beach. Only a few cars were scattered among the spaces, hopefully a sign that she wouldn't cross paths with anyone.

Heeding Officer Hensley's advice, she left the top up and carried her supper to the empty picnic table near the trees. Andria would have a conniption if she knew about the greasy burger and homemade chips on the menu, but her mac-and-cheese bribe yesterday was no better. Did she really think a high-carb, high-fat carrot would convince any sane person to support her career decision? How could she work with someone like Lucas Calloway?

Roma sat on the table facing her car, the carryout container on her lap and her feet resting on the bench seat. Barry's red sheen reflected the afternoon sunlight and brightened her mood with the deep infatuation he always triggered. *You're the only one who'll ever own my heart.*

A gooey blob of cheese dripped onto her chips as she bit into the meaty goodness of her sandwich. Flavors burst on her taste buds, the mix of beef, bacon, barbecue sauce, and cheese almost as orgasmic as the sexual kind. *And you're a close second to Barry.*

A squirrel eyed her from several feet away, clearly thinking he could beg her into sharing. She scooped the melty mess with a pair of chips and stuffed it in her mouth. "Mmm. This is all mine, Rocky, so go eat a nut."

"A Rocky and Bullwinkle fan?"

The familiar voice tempted her to set aside her meal and drop kick the invader of her personal space into next week. *Or drag him into the woods and fuck him senseless.* "Stalking me so you can apologize, Calloway?"

"You answer my question and I'll answer yours." He lifted one trainer-clad foot to the table, inches from her hip, and extended his head and arms toward her. Perspiration dribbled down well-defined biceps and darkened the royal-blue muscle shirt clinging to his back. His sweat-soaked hair stood out every which way and a droplet rolled into the untrimmed razor stubble lining his jaw and upper lip as he glanced up at her from his stretch.

Lord, have mercy. "Only the original." She stuffed another bite of sandwich in her mouth to keep from drooling.

"Me too. I'm pretty sure I was here first, so maybe you're stalking me." He lowered his hairy leg and switched to the other side. His fingertips brushed her thigh, inciting goose bumps and a flutter in her lower belly. "You're horny and I'm handy?"

She gave him one of her sister's down-the-nose looks and shook her head. "I can take care of myself if I'm horny."

"Where's the fun in that?"

CHAPTER 10

"A vibrator doesn't complain when I put it in my dresser drawer when I'm done with it." Roma glanced downward, breaking eye contact and urging his cock to fight the constraints of the net lining in his shorts. "I doubt you can say that about yourself and the likelihood that you have a condom in those running shorts seems improbable. You also didn't answer my real question."

A dab of barbecue sauce on her lower lip invited Lucas to lick it off, but he used his finger to wipe her skin clean instead and sucked off the sweet-and-spicy smear. Her breath hitched, sending another jolt to his dick. "Why should I apologize for Glenn's mistake? My actions were based on the paperwork he gave me. It wasn't personal."

"It was just you being a jerk then." She paused with a cheese-covered chip near her mouth. "Crush the small-business owner to make a buck. I may not be sweet, but I wouldn't go that far."

He shrugged. "I didn't do anything illegal, and the purpose of buying out Glenn was to have three empty storefronts for Foundation projects. He pulled a fast one on both of us. FYI, I never run without my wallet. Gotta have ID and other necessities, in case of an emergency."

"Emergency? Right. He pulled a fast one on *you*. It's all good as far as I'm concerned since my lease protects me." The sandwich shrank by a third with her next bite.

"Are you willing to discuss a mutually satisfying arrangement?"

She chugged half a bottle of water before meeting his gaze again. It held the usual dose of annoyance and sarcasm. "Your dick will still be there when I'm done eating."

"I meant business, but that works too. Lots of cover in the woods. Or my truck's parked over there." He pointed to the far end at the opposite side of the lot as he sat facing her on the bench next to her feet. The position hid his erection, even if it wasn't terribly comfortable. Watching her eat only added to the discomfort, but a little patience and a hard-on wouldn't kill him.

"You're staring." She shoveled in a chip loaded with more of the fallen toppings from her burger.

"Yes."

"Shtop it." Her full-mouthed lisp proved she didn't give a damn about trying to impress him, making her an anomaly. She also hadn't asked the question most women would have posed, either—why.

"No." The wild curls escaping the messy knot atop her head dared him to remove the bandana she wore like a headband and whatever else tied her hair in place.

She glared at him, but her quick temper only multiplied his desire to get her naked. "You're an annoying ass."

"When it works to my advantage. I'm trying to figure out what makes you tick." Analyzing why he was drawn to her would go a long way in solving the problem of how to forget her. He'd have enough regrets to deal with when he left town without having a woman on his mind.

"That ticking is the timer on my temper, and it's counting down to zero."

"Save it for our adventure in the woods. Sex is pretty spectacular when you're pissed off at me." He feathered his fingertips down her calf. His reward was half a moan and a slap on the hand.

"You're remarkably easy to be pissed off at." She popped the final bite of the sandwich in her mouth, but a few chips remained in the carryout box.

"Are you going eat those?"

"Yes, and I'm not sharing them with you."

"Actually, I was wondering if you're ready to go exploring. I need to shower before my five-o'clock appointment." *Time to poke the badger again.* "And, no, it isn't a date."

On cue, her brown eyes darkened, hinting at a new level of fury as she set aside the box. "I'm not the one who suggested having sex in the woods. You can always leave without it if you're in such a goddamn hurry."

"You don't want my cock inside you? Because it most definitely wants to be there." He ducked his head and lifted her leg over him as he slid to the left. The position would have put her pussy within licking range if not for her shorts. "If we were someplace less public, I'd eat you while you—"

"Stop talking." Her belly muscles shuddered in front of him, contradicting her words and her bossy tone.

"Or what? You'll come right here and now?" He grinned up at her. "That would be an interesting development to say the least. What do think will happen when I actually touch you?"

"You'll get a knee to the groin if you don't shut your mouth." She crammed in the last handful of chips and reached for the bottled water.

"You'd try to damage the part of me that gives you the most pleasure?" He chanced a slow lick along her inner thigh from her knee to the ragged hem of her cutoffs. "Or is it my tongue that makes you feel good?"

Her choked growl might have warned him off if it hadn't ended with an uninhibited moan. In a few efficient motions, she packed up the trash from her meal and swung her leg over his head. "Woods. Now."

Snagging the carryout bag and closing his hand around her smaller one, he climbed out of the bench seat. Rather than jerking out of his grasp, she led him away from the picnic table and to the trail leading into the trees. Shade closed around them, blocking out the bright sunlight but not the sweltering heat. Most of it stemmed from the need to find release with her.

Maybe Andria was right. He liked Roma, despite her abrasive personality—or possibly because of it. Her complete lack of pretense ensured no games, no tricks, and no false affection.

No future, either.

That realization lit a spark of disappointment, but she stepped off the path and weaved past several large trees before he could snuff it out on his own. "Condom."

He'd barely retrieved it from his wallet when she halted and shed her shorts and underwear. The sight sent his heart thumping in his chest, the way it might have when he was a teenager—if he'd had any experience stealing away into the woods with a girl at that age. Even giving up his virginity at twenty-three hadn't approached what Roma Denata did to him.

"Are you just going to stand there staring all day? Suit up, or I'm out of here, Calloway." Her scowl said it wasn't an idle threat.

He freed his dick and donned the protection, unsure how his selective process of choosing sex partners had failed him fifteen years later. Although her interest in non-committal sex made her the perfect accomplice, she was nothing like his usual type, and five consecutive days of banging each other wasn't his MO.

"On the ground." She tugged on his shirt and dropped to her knees. "I hear voices."

Following her instructions, he stretched out on the forest floor, glad he wasn't bare-assed on the sticks and stones beneath him. Not getting caught would be a good thing too.

Then she straddled his hips and sank onto his cock, driving the air from his lungs. Her low groan echoed the one in his head, and he guided her mouth to his to keep from voicing his pleasure aloud. Thrusting in time with the rhythm she set, he met her tongue and her pussy in unison. Every stroke dragged him toward an explosive escape, even as the voices grew closer.

A dog barked, warning him to freeze, but she drove her body against his. The rapid squeeze-and-release motion on his dick signaled her impending orgasm, offering him no choice but to surrender to his body's demand to join her.

She squeaked into his mouth as she trembled above him, and he fought a roar when the pressure burst up his length from his testicles. Her lips and tongue continued their aggressive assault with another violent tremor through her muscles, pulling him along in the wake of her ongoing orgasm.

Rough breathing bathed his neck in humidity for several long seconds after the voices and barking faded. Then she pushed upward, grabbing for her clothes as she stood. Without a word or a backward glance, she dressed, picked up her trash, and took off toward the hiking trail. Her orange tank and matching bandana shone through the trees all the way to the trailhead.

He'd always been the first to leave, to escape before the woman could pose the questions he didn't want to have to answer. No, he wasn't interested in a relationship. No, he didn't want to see her again. No, sex didn't mean he had feelings for her.

Those answers would have been the truth with every other female he'd ever known.

He tucked his deflating latex-encased dick in his shorts and, still reeling from another monumental fuck with Roma, brushed the loose twigs and dirt from the back of his clothes. As brusque and cold-hearted as she was, Roma deserved better than a man with his past, not that she seemed to let anyone close enough to really know her.

Using each other for sex. That's how her sister had described their series of encounters. She couldn't have been more right about that.

Enemies one minute and lovers the next.

That they'd done it multiple times concerned him more.

What the hell am I doing?

Roma's car was gone when he entered the clearing near the parking lot, true to her fuck-and-run form. Too bad it left an ache in the pit of his stomach.

Maybe Andria had also seen what he hadn't recognized or acknowledged in the short time he'd known Roma. The feeling was too familiar for her to have planted the idea in his brain this morning. He enjoyed, looked forward even, to sparring with her sister, knowing it would end with sexual satisfaction until they met again.

The drive to his apartment and a hot shower gave him more opportunity to fixate on the attraction, when they should have cleared his mind. As he dressed, a disconcerting thought popped to the forefront. For all his deliberate baiting, he hadn't teased her with his perpetual "short stuff" insult today. Seeing her sitting on the picnic table like she'd been waiting for him had thrown him off kilter.

His phone buzzed against the counter twice in quick succession when he returned to the kitchen, pulling him from the hormone-induced fog. He grabbed his keys and picked up his cell, hoping for a message from his lawyer or accountant and any reason to leave town for a few days, anything to stop the cycle.

Bobby's name and number lit up the screen with a message about canceling their plan to meet for wings and a beer. Relief far outweighed disappointment since the get-together promised rehashing best-forgotten events from school. Lucas tapped in a suitable response that suggested they would try again later in the week.

Before he could pocket his phone, it vibrated again, this time with a text from his mother.

"Do you have time to stop by the office? I'd like your opinion on an idea. Or I can drop in at the center. Whatever's convenient for you."

Only an outright lie would get him off the hook, even though a visit didn't sound half bad after Roma's hasty post-sex desertion. *"Already left the center. How about if I come by the house after supper?"*

"Have supper with us? Your dad's picking up pizza on the way home from the grocery store. I was just about to order. Mediterranean veggie and supreme okay? Breadsticks? Salad?" Her bribery skills evidently hadn't gotten rusty in the years since he'd left home.

"Perfect." It wasn't, but what choice did he have? *"See you soon."*

"Home in about fifteen minutes. :)"

He ignored the impulse to pack a bag and put some distance between him and the place he still called home. His mom would chase him down eventually, in his conscience or in person.

Luckily, the drive took him in the opposite direction of Roma's Gourmet Gelato, but he couldn't escape the woman's presence in his head. Depriving himself of sex the last several months would have been a reasonable explanation for the lapse if he'd kept to his limit of three times per partner. Five times was unprecedented, and he'd made no attempt to resist going back for more.

He parked beneath the oak tree, the sinking feeling in his insides warning him of a major miscalculation. Staying wasn't an option, but why did that fact bother him this time?

The creek behind the house pulled him toward the spot where he'd spent hours venting his anger as a kid—on Bobby's behalf and his own. The slope down the bank seemed less steep now and the creek had been wider and deeper to his ten-year-old self. The trees had spread toward the sky, shading much of the gurgling stream.

He kicked off his shoes and carefully stepped into the rocky shallows. The water cooled his bare feet, soothing some of the frustration from his association with Roma. She was a lot like the creek—fluctuating temperament, sharp rocks amid smooth stones, unpredictable. Damned if she didn't drown him in pleasure too.

"I thought I'd find you here." His mom followed the same path down the hill and slipped off her sandals next to his. "This was your favorite place to disappear to. Your dad always told me you'd be fine, but I couldn't help checking on you. Mothers worry, even when their children are grown."

Bracing his feet on the slippery rocks, he offered her his hand. "You brought snacks so I wouldn't think you were making sure I didn't fall in and break a leg. You don't come down here by yourself, do you?"

"Reversing roles, are you?" She squeezed his hand and leaned her head against his shoulder. "Maybe you'd worry less if you lived closer."

"I promise to think about it." He hadn't thought about much else since he'd sublet his current living quarters on a month-to-month basis. Water rippled over his toes, easing some of the tension the topic never failed to trigger.

"We should head up to the house. Your dad'll be home any minute."

He guided her back to their shoes, thankful she hadn't pushed harder for him to stay. His answer probably wouldn't have been what she wanted to hear.

Halfway across the backyard, she glanced toward him. "You and Andria seem to be working well together."

Fairly certain of her intent, he shook his head. "She's good at what she does. That's why I interviewed her."

"Have you thought about—"

"We're just colleagues. She asked for part of the day off tomorrow because she and her ex-husband are getting remarried."

His mom tsked as she ascended the steps to the deck off the kitchen. "That's not what I was going to say. You're way too uncommunicative for someone like Andria."

"I talk when it's important." He followed her inside, wishing he'd never agreed to stay for supper.

"Sometimes. Sometimes not. Would you mind setting the table?" At the pantry, she withdrew a stack of paper plates. "So the idea I have. What do you think about providing support for people indirectly affected by rape? Parents, spouses, significant others, children, friends of victims."

"Andria already has it on her list." *Please don't make this about me.*

"Good. I'm guessing she and her husband are back together because they went to counseling recently. What if they'd done it four years ago?" She set bowls and forks on the counter. "For the salad. You would've benefited from that kind of help too, but…"

Turning his back to her, he swallowed the retort on the tip of his tongue. "I think I hear the garage door. I'll go see if Dad needs help carrying in the groceries."

CHAPTER 11

Roma shoved open the service entrance with her hip and lugged the empty boxes to the recycle bin. As she raised her fist to break out the bottom of the first box, familiar laughter from the rear parking lot stopped her in her tracks.

Andria and Lucas walked side by side toward the building next door, his hand at the small of her back and her sister smiling broader than she had in years. She'd been in the bathroom when Roma had asked about riding into work together and had told her to go ahead, that she'd drive herself. The summery dress and heels spoke of a woman trying to impress a man, which her sister had clearly intended to hide from her.

And Lucas. His Jekyll-and-Hyde personality was the mark of someone who couldn't be trusted.

Leaving the boxes, Roma stormed back into the shop for her phone. A private meeting with Andria was in order, one that revealed his true nature. Then she'd rake Calloway over the coals until his dick was permanently flaccid.

After a check on the four operating churns, she turned toward her office. Halfway there, a knock sounded on the back door.

You saved me a text message. She detoured to the service entrance and flung it open. "I warned you about him."

Lucas stood framed in the doorway, his casual stance and tailored suit masking his lack of ethics. His left eyebrow rose a fraction of an inch, adding to her outrage as he moved toward her. "You wouldn't be talking about me, would you?"

"Of course I am." She cursed herself for taking a backward step and allowing him into her kitchen. "What do you want?"

"Pleasant greeting. Good morning to you too." He slipped his hands in his pockets as he nudged the door closed with a wingtip. "We never got around to our business discussion yesterday."

"Other than paying rent, I'm not doing business with the likes of you." Letting her hellfire mood take control, she grabbed the messy ladle from her worktable and pointed at his chest. "Stay the hell away from my sister."

A self-important grin spread across his face. "Do I detect a hint of jealousy?"

She snorted and shook the utensil at him, sending drips sailing to the floor but missing him. "You wish. I'm giving you fair warning. She's off-limits to your type."

"My type, huh?" He held his ground, even though common sense should've chased him out of town. "What exactly is my type? Sexy? Irresistible?"

She narrowed her eyes. "You know damn well what I mean. If you touch Andria, they'll never find your body."

"That sounds like a threat."

"It's a promise. Go fuck a fence post if you can't keep your dick in your pants."

His insolent laugh tempted her to whack him upside the head. "Too many splinters. What if I'd rather fuck you? Again."

"Fuck me all you want, but you stay away from her." She stabbed the ladle at him, but she maintained her distance. "She's been hurt enough."

"What about your feelings?"

Rage singed her insides. She swapped the ladle for the empty gelato-mix container beside her and heaved it at him. "I'd have to have feelings for them to be hurt."

He didn't even flinch as the bucket whirred past his head and clattered to the floor. Pieces ricocheted every which way.

"I should've hit you smack dab in that sanctimonious sneer instead of giving you a warning." She jerked her tank top and sports bra over her head and stripped off her shorts and underwear, leaving her naked in front of him. "I thought you wanted to fuck me."

His jaw twitched, but he turned his back to her and reached for the doorknob. "I do, but I'm not going to."

Panic ripped through her gut with the knowledge that he planned to pursue her sister and Andria was too damn naïve to see what a bastard he was. "Just so you know, I'm willing to go to jail for her. And if you think I'm kidding, try me. I dare you."

Without a word or a backward glance, the worm slunk out the service entrance and closed it behind him.

She hurled the ladle at the metal door. "*Bugiardo, cornutazzo, puttaniere di merda*!"

The timer beeped for the first churn, but a well-aimed swing sent it crashing into the wall. The slimy womanizing son of a bitch would regret being born when she finished with him.

She switched off the churn and headed to the walk-in fridge for another flavor of mix, dodging gelato puddles and bits of plastic bucket. Icy air bit her nipples before she even walked inside, a stark reminder of her nudity.

"Damn it all to hell." Changing directions, she returned to the pile of clothing next to a splatter of pink goo to dress. None of it would've happened if Andria had ridden with her to work. "And now I have to clean up this mess. Karma isn't the only bitch around here, Calloway."

The disorder might drive her nuts, but sweeping and mopping would have to wait until she started the second round of churning. She transferred the finished batch of strawberry to a serving pan, washed the churn parts, and retrieved the next bucket of mix.

The buzz of the delivery bell rang through the kitchen as she scooped gelato mix into the clean canister and fit the lid onto the stem of the paddle. She wasn't expecting a shipment and Tess wouldn't arrive for at least two hours. If her landlord had the balls to show up again, she'd have to close the shop—because she would more than likely end up in jail for assaulting him. "Go the fuck away."

More buzzing grated on her last nerve.

Growling at the interruption, she crossed to the service entrance and checked the peephole before swinging the door wide. Her sister stood outside, concern marring her otherwise perfect face. At least Calloway hadn't returned to test her willpower.

"Don't I get a hello?" Andria picked up the cracked container at her feet and followed the trail of scattered pieces and gelato-mix drips toward the walk-in cooler. "What happened in here?"

"Nothing." Roma shoved the loose strands of hair falling in her face back under the bandana around her head. "Aren't you supposed to be working? Or is your boss giving you preferential treatment."

"Lovely to see you too, sis." Andria's disapproving frown had become all too familiar lately. "I was hoping you have a few minutes to talk. I have some news I want to share."

Adjusting her hold on the ladle, Roma dunked it into the batch of mango-vanilla bean mix. The urge to throw it still lingered, but she focused on her task. "I already know about you and your new boyfriend."

"Who told you?"

"Give me a little credit. It wasn't exactly hard to figure out."

"Do you also know I'm moving out today?"

Metal clanked against metal as Roma lost her grip on the ladle. "*Moving out?* Why? I know I can be a bear to get along with, but—"

"This has nothing to do with you. I can't even begin to repay you for being there when I needed you." Andria paced to the prep table and back to the cooler. "Matt and I are getting remarried this afternoon."

"*Matt?*" Roma's stomach dropped to the floor, along with the utensil. "What about— That bastard left you!"

"He left because I pushed him away. I told him to leave. We're both to blame for our marriage falling apart. He couldn't deal with what happened to me and I shut him out, but we never stopped loving each other. It's time to put the past behind us and be together again. Three and a half years is a long time to be unhappy."

"And how long has this been going on behind my back?" She tossed the ladle in the sink, relishing the racket it caused.

"I'm not a baby. I don't owe you an explanation and I don't need your permission. You should be happy for me."

Roma crossed her arms under her breasts and leveled a glare at Andria. "How long?"

Her sister walked to the sink and turned on the faucet. Droplets splattered all directions when she held the tool under the stream of water. "We've been seeing each other and going to counseling together for about six months."

"*Six months?* And you *just* decided to tell me? How could you keep secrets from me?" The guilty conscience Andria had never learned to hide stared Roma in the face. "Oh my God, all those times you said you had to go out of town and house sit. You *lied* to me."

Andria turned away, clearly feeling too ashamed of her deception to look Roma in the eye. "What was I supposed to do? You would've freaked out if you knew I was seeing Matt, but he isn't the bad guy. You aren't in charge of my life, Roma, and you're not responsible for it. It's time for you to move on too."

"Move on? I have a life, and I'm perfectly happy with it." Roma lifted a clean ladle from its wall hook and lowered it into the fragrant mango mix.

"Are you?" Andria shuffled to the exit, sighing as she paused with her hand on the doorknob. "I wish you could forgive yourself. Actually, there's nothing to forgive. Nobody ever blamed you, except you."

Every muscle in Roma's body seized, cramping tighter when the door closed with her sister on the other side. Pain radiated from every nerve and amplified with every passing second. Her throat smarted from the urge to shriek at the top of her lungs, but she couldn't push it out of her mouth. The sound was frozen inside her. Nearly half a decade of anger was frozen inside her with it.

Why can't I just explode and make it all go away?

The crippling ache spread to every inch of her, inside and out, stealing her breath and blotting out her vision.

I will not pass out. I will not pass out. I will not fucking pass out.

She finally released her grip on the ladle, not caring if it sank into the depths of the tub, and slumped to the floor. Tingles spread through her limbs as she forced slow inhales and exhales. Each breath cleared her vision a little more and eased the throbbing pain in her body, but the attack on her psyche didn't abate.

It's my fault. I should've seen what he was. How could I have been so blind?

The words and images that had been carved into her mind the afternoon she walked in on her fiancé assaulting Andria hadn't worn away with time. They stood out like thick scabs. Scars had formed over the wounds, but the tissue beneath never healed, no matter how much time passed.

Forgive? How can I?

She squeezed her eyes shut and let the flashing colors and shapes take over her thoughts. Forgetting was easier, at least for a little while. Then she would throw herself into her work to block out the memories and rely on her anger to get her through another week, another month, another year. She'd survived four years of being chased by demons using that method.

I'll be damned if they're catching me now.

A full minute of flexing her hands and feet rid her fingers and toes of the tingling sensation enough to stand. She swayed from the lingering lightheadedness, but the wall provided all the support she needed. It was solid and immoveable, exactly the kind of wall she preferred. Nothing and no one could get in.

Cleaning the kitchen within an inch of its life soothed most of Roma's anxiety, but she mopped the dining area and loaded the freezer case to avoid thinking about going home to an empty house. Knowing Lucas Calloway hadn't laid his disgusting paws on Andria offered more consolation than Roma liked, even if Matt wasn't a much better choice than that despicable clod.

She yanked harder than necessary on the cords to open the front blinds and nearly jumped out of her skin when a man peered back at her from the other side of the glass. His beady eyes and comb-over seemed vaguely familiar. Then he held up a Medina County Health Department ID tag.

The creep who gets pissy when he can't find a violation. You could eat off my floors this morning, so good luck screwing with my perfect record, chump.

Pasting on a passive expression, she unlocked the door and ushered him inside. "Unannounced inspection, I presume?"

He grunted and stepped past her. "We received a complaint."

"Excuse me?" She bit her cheek to keep from demanding to know who had the nerve to submit a phony grievance against her business.

"Take a seat while I look around." Clipboard in hand, he surveyed the service areas on his way to the kitchen.

Her temper once again seething, she followed his instructions, certain he'd manufacture a violation if she didn't. *I will find out who you are and you will pay.*

Several minutes passed before he reappeared. His grimace suggested he'd come up empty-handed again and wasn't particularly pleased about it. He walked to the front entrance and pulled two papers from the clipboard. Her stomach knotted as he taped one to the glass and set the other on the closest table. "You have a rodent infestation. I'll be back in seven days for a follow-up inspection. Until you correct the violation, you're closed for business."

She pushed out of the chair, sending it crashing backward. "Like hell I have an infestation! What kind of rodents?"

He scowled in her direction and grabbed the door handle. "I found two dead mice in the storeroom and another under the sink in the kitchen."

"I just cleaned every surface in the kitchen an hour ago. There weren't any mice anywhere, dead or alive." *You lying snake!*

Stepping onto the sidewalk, he smirked at her over his shoulder. "You can fix the problem or I can shut you down for good. One week."

She stalked to the kitchen, too angry to even acknowledge the crooked SOB. "Rodents, my ass. The only question is whether you did this on your own or somebody put you up to it."

A rigid mouse no bigger than her thumb lay under the sink in plain sight, an impossibility after her thorough floor scrubbing of the space right before his arrival. Both critters in the supply closet were clearly visible from the doorway, also confirming that she couldn't have missed seeing them.

What motive did the inspector have for planting dead vermin in her restaurant?

Motive. Son of a scum-sucking prick. The only rat to visit her kitchen was her landlord.

The service entrance banged shut behind her as she stormed next door. After trying the knob and finding it locked, she pounded on the only thing standing between her and retribution against her landlord.

A chorus of vicious barking warned her Maxine had heard the noise loud and clear. The door cracked open and Andria poked her head through a narrow slit. "It's okay, Maxine. Good girl. Roma, what are you doing? Trying to wake the dead?"

"Where is he?" Pushing past her sister and Maxine, Roma marched toward Lucas's office. At least this time she wouldn't have any trouble resisting temptation. "Where are you, you pig?"

"He left for a meeting over an hour ago."

She whirled around, angrier still that she had no one to punish. "That bastard called the health department for a bogus rodent violation and got me shut down!"

"Shut down?" The color drained from Andria's cheeks. "He wouldn't do that."

"Wouldn't he? Oh, I forgot. You know him much better than I do." Roma rolled her eyes and skirted her sister as she returned to the rear exit. "Did he tell you why he wants my building? And that he wanted to discuss a *business arrangement* with me?"

"Yes, I know why and I also know what he wanted to discuss with you." Andria followed her to the door. "You're so off-base with that accusation."

"My instincts say otherwise. He couldn't kick me out with my lease, so he had the damn inspector plant mice in my kitchen. Blackmail, bribery. I don't know which, but I'll prove it before you get home tonigh—" The sudden realization that she wouldn't see her sister at home stung, and she hurried outside to escape it. "Never mind."

"Roma!"

She plowed through the back entrance and locked it behind her. Ringing from her office carried into the room, but she had no interest in listening to Andria's rationalizations if she had the gall to try to explain away her traitorous actions.

Thankfully, Tess's name lit up the screen. Even so, Roma let the call go to voicemail, sank into the chair at her desk, and dropped her head into her shaking hands. When the buzz of the delivery bell echoed through the kitchen, she moved her fingers to her ears, hoping to block out the sound.

A muted *ding* penetrated the barrier and her phone lit up again, this time with a text from Tess. *"Just found out I have to attend orientation for my internship the first week of August and start the next week. Please don't be mad, but I'm giving my two weeks' notice. :("*

CHAPTER 12

Leaning back in the driver's seat, Lucas rubbed the tense muscles in his neck and mentally reviewed the calendar for the rest of his day. The stark image of Roma standing naked in front of him resurfaced again, the unspoken desperation in her eyes cutting deeper than the acid in her blatant threats. He shouldn't have taunted her, but the only other option would've been to admit the feelings he had were for *her*, not her sister.

I never should've agreed to run this project.

He could be off somewhere, making money hand over fist and pretending he was happy with his life. No ties and no commitments had served him well for twenty years. Why the hell did it have to change now?

His phone vibrated against his leg, and he stretched to shove his hand in his pocket to retrieve it. Andria's name on the screen set off a battle of whether or not to answer the call.

Damn it. "Calloway."

"Hi, Lucas. I'm not interrupting, am I? You said your meeting would be over by noon."

"It's fine. I finished five minutes ago. I'm picking up some lunch on my way to the center. Can I get something for you?" He started the engine and set aside his cell when the Bluetooth kicked on through the truck.

"I brought lunch, but thanks for the offer. I need to ask you a question, not that I'm accusing you or anything. I just want to hear it directly from you." The hesitation in her voice put his senses on high alert.

He merged into the lane of traffic headed toward the north side of town. "Go ahead."

A heavy sigh warned him it probably had something to do with her sister. "Did you file a complaint with the health department against Roma's Gourmet Gelato?"

"What?" Signaling to change lanes, he replayed the question in his mind. "I haven't even eaten there. Why the hell would I do that?"

"Yes or no."

"No, I haven't complained to the health department about Roma. Why would you think that?" A sinking feeling joined the rumbling in his stomach. "Is she making up shit stories about me?"

"An inspector found mice in her kitchen and shut her down this morning, and she thinks you paid him to put them there. You tried to break the lease, so she assumed…"

"The worst." Ignoring his appetite, he switched on his turn signal and made a left to take him around the block and toward downtown. "I'll be there in five minutes."

"Lucas?"

"Yeah?"

"Please try to understand her point of view. You threatened to evict her."

"I made a mistake." He embraced the surge of guilt her reminder inspired. "She has every right to suspect me. I don't know who did this, but I'm going to find out."

"Okay. See you in a few minutes."

The line went silent, but his brain made up for the lack of conversation, unable to discard any names from his short list of possible grudge-holders. Roma's penchant for speaking her mind wasn't exactly an endearing quality to anyone.

Except maybe to Uncle Glenn.

He parked in his usual spot behind the trio of storefronts, noting the absence of her 'Cuda named Barry, where they'd almost been caught having sex in the backseat. His unanswered knock on the rear entrance didn't necessarily confirm she wasn't at the shop, so he jogged to the front of the building. The Medina County Health Department notice taped to the glass yanked the knot in his stomach tighter, but the dark —and empty—serving area sparked more anger than he'd felt in a long time.

Before he reached the reception desk next door, Andria appeared in her office doorway with Maxine at her side. "This couldn't have happened at a worse time. She was already upset because I'm moving out today. And her reaction when I told her Matt and I are getting remarried… I kept our reconciliation a secret in case it didn't work out, but she accused me of lying to her, which I suppose is true. Anyway, I can't imagine how devastated she is."

He gestured for her to follow him into the room he'd claimed, hoping to keep his self-control intact. At the desk, he withdrew the box with the engraved picture frame he'd placed in the bottom drawer during her lunch break yesterday. "For you and Matt. Congratulations. You should get going so you're on time for the wedding. I'll do what I can about the health department and check on Roma."

Andria enveloped him in a hug much like the ones his mom bestowed upon him, the same gentle warmth and understanding seeping into his soul. As she stepped back, she brushed a tear from her cheek. "Thank you. For the present and for helping my sister. She's lucky to have you."

His shrug earned him a smile before she picked up the package and left his office with her companion. Even in the off chance Roma wanted him, he hadn't given himself to her and wasn't sure he could if he wanted to.

Do I want to?

An hour of scouring the internet and three phone calls later, he finally surrendered to his need for food. His efforts hadn't produced the immediate results he'd hoped for, but his inquiries had gained enough information to support digging deeper.

Lunch first.

Not trusting his luck with the front-door locks, he went out the back way, wishing he'd ditched his suit coat half a block from the center. Sweat trickled down his spine as he waited for the light to change.

"Good day for gelato, don't you think? Too bad some jerk targeted Roma and got her shut down."

Turning toward the man who'd joined him at the crosswalk, Lucas nodded, fairly certain of the guy's implication. "Yeah."

"You're her new landlord, aren't you? Ben Kaiser. Her lawyer."

How can I work this to my advantage? Lucas offered his hand and a business card to Roma's legal representative as the light changed. "Lucas Calloway. Join me for lunch?"

Moving up to walk beside him, Kaiser shook Lucas's hand and took the card. "Sure, but you should know she'll never agree to new terms and I'd be a fool to advise her to do so."

"No worries, Ben. I have other plans."

"Like driving her out of business?"

Lucas shot a glare at the lawyer as they turned toward the café. "I had nothing to do with the health department bullshit. It's obvious somebody's got an ax to grind. Any ideas who might want to get even with her? Besides me. As I said, I have other plans."

The other man's gusty sigh didn't bode well. "That could be a long list. She hasn't made a lot of what I'd consider enemies, but she doesn't have the greatest people skills outside of her customers."

"I noticed." At the restaurant, Lucas held the door for his new acquaintance. "After you."

"Thanks." Ben's curious glances became a steady stare as they were seated and placed their orders.

Lucas took a long swallow of ice water before his proclivity for directness won out over patience. "Something on your mind?"

"A couple of things, actually." Clearing his throat, Kaiser straightened the fork and knife he'd unrolled from his napkin. "I can't help wondering what your other plans are and I want to know why you have an interest in who got Roma in trouble."

Honesty seemed like the best option, even if it was only part of the story. "You've probably heard about the rape recovery center the Calloway Foundation is funding. Roma's sister is the director and I'm working with her to get it up and running in the space north of the gelato shop. The empty storefront on the south side's going to house a self-defense studio, also subsidized by the Foundation. I'd originally planned to invest in a new business to provide job opportunities for the center's clients after Roma's lease was up, but Andria suggested talking to her about a job placement program through the center after the lease fiasco. It's more cost efficient than finding another building or set of buildings to house all three components."

"Okay. Sounds like a reasonable solution. Is Roma agreeable to the idea?"

"I've tried to talk to her about it, but she hasn't been receptive to a civilized discussion." Sex had also proven to be a significant distraction.

"She's been known to be a little stubborn."

Lucas barked a laugh. "A *little*?"

"Okay, a lot." Still fiddling with his silverware, Ben aimed a dissecting gaze at him. "I didn't put the names together before, but the Calloway Foundation… Family? What's your connection?"

"My parents created it about ten years ago with an endowment and a number of smaller donations. They asked me to oversee the new projects because of my business background." *And to try to talk me into staying.*

Ben's nod seemed to indicate the answer met with his approval. "Finding out who filed the complaint against Roma's business? What's in it for you?"

"I clear my name, since I have no doubt I'm the only suspect as far as Roma's concerned, and the job placement program can be implemented sooner." Another drink cooled the heat creeping up his neck from the inquisitive look Kaiser gave him.

"So are you and Roma…involved?"

Is it that fucking obvious? "None of your business." Lucas slid his glass to the left as the server approached with a pair of platters. The loaded burger she set in front of him looked every bit as tasty as the one Roma had devoured before their trek into the woods. "Thanks."

Ben smiled at the waitress as she delivered his grilled chicken sandwich, but he waited until she hurried toward the front of the café before speaking. "What have you done to find out who set up Roma?"

With the sandwich cupped in both hands, Lucas shook his head. "Wasted most of the last hour reading Ohio food-service code. Made a few phone calls for clarification. Nuisance complaints can be anonymous, but it's my understanding that she can hand-deliver a request for a hearing to be held within two days since it resulted in an immediate closure."

"She'll be breathing fire in two days, and a hearing won't replace her lost income. We need to help her reopen ASAP."

We? Maybe having a lawyer helping with the problem isn't a bad idea. "Andria mentioned Roma thinking I paid the inspector to put mice in her kitchen. What if somebody else did?"

Kaiser lowered his sandwich to the plate and furrowed his brow. "Bribery and influencing a public official are serious charges. I'm not as familiar with that area of law, but the inspector would lose his or her job, at the very least, for accepting a bribe and falsifying a report. The health department would probably conduct a new inspection. The person trying to influence might be charged with a misdemeanor. Possibly a fine or restitution."

"So if someone admitted to—"

"Hold it right there." Although the restaurant wasn't particularly busy, Ben leaned forward and lowered his voice. "You're not confessing to a crime you didn't commit to save Roma from a crooked inspector. I took an oath to uphold the law and I'll step forward with the truth if I'm put in that position."

"Do you have a better idea?" Lucas finally bit into his burger to keep from letting loose of string of expletives sure to get him thrown out of the café.

"Yes. The first step is to have her submit a request for a hearing.

I'll call her as soon as we're done here and get the ball rolling on that angle. More than likely, she isn't aware of the appeal process. Then we gather the facts and decide where to go from there. And so we're on the same page, jail is *not* the destination." Kaiser shook his head and picked up his sandwich again. "I'm getting the impression you're as short-tempered as Roma."

"Not even close. I've never screamed at her in Italian, or English for that matter." The sweet-salty-tangy-spicy flavor of the burger toppings made him wish he could sample a dribble of barbecue sauce from Roma's lip again. "She's one of a kind."

"Yes, she is, so be careful with her. And if you're going to be part of this fact-finding mission, you have to play by my rules." The man's innocuous expression turned stern. "We're trying to fix the problem, not make it worse. Under no circumstances are you to talk to the inspector, if we can even find out who he or she is. Agreed?"

"I don't like it, but okay. For now." The messy burger dripped onto the house-made chips, handing Lucas yet another reminder of yesterday's outdoor tryst.

As Kaiser chewed, his warning gaze locked on Lucas's. "I'm holding you to that promise. Question. Did you see or talk to Roma this morning before the inspection?"

A curt nod was all Lucas could manage. Her accusation still left a bitter taste in his mouth.

"What time were you there? How would you describe her mood? What was the condition of the shop when you were there? Clean? Dirty? Normal preparation kind of messy?"

"About eight thirty." A drink of water did little to clear the hard lump from his throat. "We argued, which is typical. The churns were running, but the kitchen was clean—until she threw a bucket at me."

Ben's eyebrows twitched upward, the only sign of surprise. "What did you argue about?"

"She told me to stay away from Andria and I asked her if she was jealous. I probably shouldn't have baited her, but neither of us gave her any reason to think we're anything other than business associates with a purely professional relationship."

"What happened then?"

No way in hell would he tell anyone about refusing her proposition. It had taken every ounce of self-discipline he possessed to walk away. "We argued some more and I left."

"And what was the condition of the kitchen when you left? Did you see any mice?"

"No mice. There were pieces of plastic on the floor from the broken bucket and some drips from the ladle she was swinging around. I heard something else crash right after I went out the rear entrance. Maybe the ladle against the steel door? I had a meeting at nine and my truck was in the back parking lot."

"Did you see her again after that?"

"No, but Andria did. She went over to tell Roma she was moving out and remarrying her ex-husband today."

Ben froze with a pickle spear almost to his mouth. "No kidding? Good for them. I bet Roma isn't happy about it, though."

"Understatement, according to Andria. After the inspection, Roma came to the center, wanting my head on a platter. Luckily, I was still in a meeting at the Foundation offices. Andria called me as I was getting ready to head back to the center." Pushing his mostly empty plate away, Lucas signaled the waitress for the check. "I know my previous actions paint me as the bad guy, but there are some lines I just don't cross."

"Then do exactly what I say. Stay away from the inspector and keep your eyes and ears open for leads. I'll call you later." Kaiser slid his card and some cash across the table as he stood. "That should cover my lunch and the tip. Oh, and stop playing games with Roma. Either you admit you have feelings for her or leave her alone."

CHAPTER 13

Leaves rustled in a solitary breeze, making slivers of moonlight dance on the hood of Lucas's truck. It didn't calm his nerves or prepare him for the confrontation he'd put off during the twenty minutes he'd been sitting in Roma's driveway. Another hour, day, or week wouldn't make a difference, either. He'd learned long ago to face the inevitable head on since delaying often compounded the issue. Kaiser's update had forced his hand.

Lucas pulled the keys from the ignition and slipped out the door with barely a sound, never taking his eyes off the lamp-lit windows of the first-floor sunroom. Shadowy outlines of hanging plants blocked much of his view, but she was there. A shapely silhouette had moved across the room several times while he'd talked himself into and out of knocking on the front door a dozen times.

Then she'd vanished among the spidery plants and vines as the light had dimmed but not quite gone out. Most likely, she sat in the near darkness, still fuming over the closure of her shop and Andria's decision to move out and remarry her ex-husband. Roma had a lot to be angry about, his ruthless pursuit of her space included.

An apology for that much wouldn't kill him.

He stuffed his keys in his pocket and walked to the front door before his insecurities kicked his ass back to the truck. Muffled chimes carried through the closed windows when he pushed the doorbell, but no one came to the door. A second time yielded the same results, so he cut through the grass to the now-dark sunroom.

You want to play games, huh? You're dealing with an expert at evasion. At the corner, he headed for the back of the house, fairly certain he'd find a patio and an exterior door. *Bingo.*

A few raps on the sliding door left him facing his own faint reflection in the glass. "Roma, open the door or I'm calling your grandma to check on you. It's the least your lover should do when you won't answer the door. I'm worried about—"

A hand clamped over his mouth from behind and something hit the backs of his knees, making them buckle. He barely managed to stay upright as he twisted away and then he wrestled his attacker to the ground.

"That call will be the last one you make, Calloway, especially after the despicable stunt you pulled today." The low hiss held as much warning as the words.

"I swear I had nothing to do with the inspection." Familiar curves aligned with his chest, belly, and crotch as Roma bucked and wiggled. Taut nipples poked at him through his T-shirt.

"Bullshit. Get off of me!"

He trapped her legs in his, shifted onto his elbows, and nibbled his captive's ear. Why had he thought he could have a civilized conversation with her? "I'd rather get you off. Want me to eat your pussy?"

Her erratic panting was interrupted by a moan, but she shook her head.

"Are you sure? I'll fuck you with my tongue and play with your clit. Or suck, whichever you prefer. I like to do both. And your nipples. Can't forget those. I promise to give your nipples plenty of attention while I go down on you."

She arched against him, pressing her hip into his erection. "Yes, damn it. Yes."

"Yes, you're sure you don't want me to?" He licked along the outer shell of her ear, captivated by the delicate part of a woman so used to pretending to be anything but utterly feminine. "Or, yes, you want me to?"

Moonlight illuminated her dark eyes and flushed cheeks, revealing the same fire she'd never been able to hide during their escapades. Indecision seemed to hover somewhere near the surface of her emotions, but she lifted her chin, evidently daring him to mock her for whatever she chose. "Want."

The gruffness in her voice said she wasn't happy about the admission, either.

He rolled to the side, taking her with him as he used the momentum to stand.

She clung to him like she expected him to drop her—one of the many challenges he had to face. "Inside. I don't want my neighbors calling the police."

With a nod, he returned to the glass door and gave it a tentative push with his elbow to test the lock. It slid freely, suggesting she'd anticipated his plan and snuck outside while he was at the front door. He would've done the same damn thing.

Cool air brushed across his face, banishing the midsummer-night humidity. The rhythmic *shoosh, shoosh, shoosh* as he entered the solarium came from a ceiling fan in the center of the room, its movement barely visible in the near darkness. He closed and locked the door as his eyes adjusted to the low light. Then he navigated his way through a maze of potted and hanging plants.

The jungle-like setting fit her personality perfectly—an Amazon warrior, despite her petite stature. A padded nest-shaped chair hung below the circling blades of the fan, drawing his immediate attention.

He weaved his way to his destination with Roma cradled high enough that she missed the vegetation. In the clear area surrounding the swing, he lowered her feet to the floor. "Is it okay if I undress you?"

Considering the self-strip-and-fuck routine they tended to follow, she surprised him by lifting her arms. "Have at it."

He lifted the hem of her tank top, allowing his fingers to skim the lower fullness of her braless breasts. "What? No argument?"

Her breath hitched, but a barely there shudder told him she'd done her best not to react. "Shut up and finish the job."

That's my Roma. Full of passion, even when she wants to hide. He couldn't deny it any longer. All he wanted was to belong to her and for her to belong to him. Maybe, with her help, he could finally acknowledge a connection to humanity.

The shirt slipped free of her body with a gentle upward tug, and he dropped it behind her. His palms met silky skin as he followed her spine to the waistband of her loose-fitting pajama shorts. They required less effort than her usual cutoffs, but working the fabric down her ass and hips instead of watching was no hardship. "That wasn't so bad, was it?"

"Fuck you." She plopped into the swing, snaked her hands up the chains, and spread her legs. Even in the dim lighting, the view was delectable.

Instead of calling her on the clichéd porn-flick pose, he kicked off his sandals and knelt between her knees. "Maybe after I feast on you."

"Maybe, huh? What happened? Is it that time of the month for you, or did your dick wear out?"

She wouldn't like his explanation, so he smoothed his hands up her toned calves and kissed her lower belly rather than answering. Her muscles trembled beneath his lips, assuring him she wasn't immune to distraction and redirection.

He brushed his stubble-roughened cheek over her inner thigh and guided her leg onto his shoulder. Her scent tried to lure him closer, but he detoured to the soft spot behind her knee. A kiss and then a nibble coaxed a breathy sigh from her. The sound touched a deeper part of him than her wild screams—somewhere in the vicinity of his heart, except in a not-quite physical sense.

Using his shoulder for leverage, she squirmed lower in the hanging nest, setting it gently swaying to and fro. Each forward motion brought his ultimate target within an inch of his face, which was surely her intent.

Instead of punishing them both with more teasing, he grasped the crisscrossing frame on the upswing to stop its momentum. Then he lowered his mouth to her pussy. The sweet-salty taste of her matched her enticing scent, drugging him as he alternately licked a path to her clit and drove his tongue inside her. He hummed his appreciation and reached for her breast with his free hand.

She arched into him as he caressed her puckered nipple with his thumb in time with flutters over the swollen bud cradled by her slick folds. Needy moans replaced angry growls mixed with shallow panting every time he retreated to the heavenly place his cock had become addicted to.

Had she ever allowed herself anything other than a wham-bam, anger-fueled fuck?

That hint of vulnerability stole his patience. Screwing him for sexual gratification might bring an orgasm, but it perpetuated the myth that she wasn't worthy of the gift he wanted to give her. She deserved more. She deserved to know she mattered to him.

He returned to her clit, ready to bring her pleasure with no expectation of his own. With each lick, he rolled her nipple between his finger and thumb, hoping she'd let go of her anger long enough to feel a few seconds of joy.

His tongue ached from lack of practice, but he sucked her clit between his teeth for a short break. *I want to give you this, Roma.*

As he tightened his hold and massaged the swollen bud with the flat of his tongue, a guttural cry erupted from her. She jerked her hips and cried out again, longer and louder. The tremors went on and on, even after her muscles went slack and her screams quieted.

Still holding onto her, he kissed her satisfied clit and the soft folds around it. Then he moved to her lower belly, her ribs, and the underside of her breast. Every inch of her tempted him to carry her off to bed and spend the whole night worshipping her body and convincing her he wanted her heart.

He slowly returned the chair to its former position, mesmerized by the look of utter contentment in her relaxed expression. Closed eyes and a hint of a smile mirrored the emotions swimming in his head. Unable to resist, he brushed his mouth along her jaw and then her sex-softened lips.

Her exhale tickled his nose as she threaded her fingers into his hair. "Bedroom. Down the hall. To the left."

He scooped her into his arms and headed toward the wide doorway leading into the house. Determined not to jump to conclusions, he willed his pulse to stay steady. "Directions? Or an invitation?"

She was quiet as they passed through the kitchen and entered the living room. Had indecision silenced her? "Turn here."

Moonlight shone in two narrow strips almost side by side across the hallway floor, guiding him toward what seemed to be a bathroom and then a bedroom on the left. He carried her into the second room and stopped beside the bed. Tangled sheets and bunched pillows spoke of a woman who slept like she had sex—with the energy of too many contradictory emotions.

He lowered her to the mattress, not holding out any hope for an invitation to join her. He would, however, stay with her, sex or not.

Rolling away from him, she stretched one leg toward the footboard and the other to the far side of the bed. She'd survived Andria moving out and remarrying the man she'd always loved today. Someone had targeted her business and forced her doors closed. Ben had called earlier to say his insistence she file an appeal had yielded a confession that her assistant manager had given notice and another employee had quit with the news of no work hours for the foreseeable future. True or not, the jealousy issue was of no consequence compared to everything else.

She flung her arm over her head, grabbed a pillow, and stuffed the misshapen bundle under her cheek. "There's a box of condoms in the nightstand drawer."

Although he would've preferred an outright invitation to stay the night, her implied enticement was a step in the right direction. He'd accept what she offered if it meant forward progress.

He stripped off his clothes, rolled on a condom, and climbed into bed beside her. Following his instincts, he curved his body along hers, not quite touching, and draped his arm around her waist. When he kissed her shoulder, she sucked in a shaky breath and tensed for a long moment, but she didn't pull away. The warrior in her evidently still waged a battle against the sated woman.

Another kiss on her neck earned him a needy whimper and she arched her ass against his erection. "Fuck me."

Hooking his elbow under her knee and easing her to her side, he vowed to do more than simply fuck her. While make love wasn't exactly the right term yet, either, it was better than the wham-bam they usually employed. For a night in her bed, he wanted slow and passionate joining, taking advantage of the hours they'd have together.

She guided his cock inside her and tried to force him deep in a single glide, but he backed off until her pussy hugged only the head. Then he eased forward, working himself along her pulsing muscles an inch at a time. Every tremor sent shockwaves to his balls and threatened to steal his control.

He closed his eyes to focus on the intoxicating scent of their joined bodies and the silkiness of her skin beneath his lips and fingertips. "God, you feel so good. I could do this for hours."

Quake after quake rumbled through her, the tension obvious in her shuddering breaths. "Faster. I'm about ready to crawl out of my fucking skin."

Pretty sure her rush to come again had more to do with her brain than her body, he surrendered to her request with deep thrusts guaranteed to get them both off in record time. Her orgasm in the jungle had been all the foreplay he needed.

A last shove sent heat flashing through his cock as she convulsed against him and filled the room with a long, throaty cry, inviting him along for the blissful ride. The physical pleasure matched their previous encounters, but she immediately rolled to her stomach and buried her head under the pillow, dulling the high as soon as it occurred.

It's no different from last time.

Standing his ground wasn't worth the risk of getting booted out of her bed. He would save that gamble for morning.

∼

Lucas yawned and reached for the woman he'd spent the entire night chasing around the bed for a fuck and a cuddle. An expanse of cool empty sheets forced his eyelids into a squint. He rubbed at the stubble covering his jaw and rolled toward the clock on the nightstand. *6:15.*

No sounds of running water or smell of coffee hinted at Roma's whereabouts while he slipped on his boxer briefs. After a quick stop in the bathroom, he headed to the sunroom. It, the living room, and the kitchen were empty, and a notepad stood propped against the coffeemaker.

"Lock up when you leave."

A harsh laugh escaped, accompanied by a pang in his chest. How many times had he slunk out of a one-night stand's bed in the wee hours to avoid the morning-after awkwardness and any possible insinuation that he could offer anything more?

Being on the receiving end, even with a woman he'd had a record number of one-offs with, stung. She'd distanced herself from him every time they'd finished making love last night, but she'd allowed him to stay, promising an eventual breakthrough in their tug-of-war relationship.

He returned to the bedroom to dress and spent ten minutes searching for his shoes. He finally found them in the sunroom, where he'd made a silent commitment to her the night before. "I'll be damned if you're getting rid of me that easily, Roma."

CHAPTER 14

Ignoring the second, more insistent buzz of the delivery bell, Roma twist-tied the bag of gelato spoons closed and tossed it on top of the cups, napkins, and cone wrappers. A scribble on the lid identified the item filling the last bit of space before she shoved the box toward the other cartons waiting to be sealed.

Scoops and ladles.

She retrieved both buckets of scoops from the freezer case and set them inside the stack of serving pans to start another box. Then she gathered the ladles from their wall hooks, relishing the way they clanged like out-of-tune bells as she moved down the row.

"You left without waking me up."

Steeling herself against Lucas's presence, she shrugged. "And you let yourself in here, when I'm clearly busy."

"You're packing."

"Obviously."

"Why? Did the health department deny you a hearing?" The outrage in his voice threatened to slice through the armor she'd scrambled to put on.

She slid the sheaf of papers she'd assembled toward the end of the worktable. A tingle along her spine suggested he'd moved closer, but she kept her eyes averted. "This is notice that I'm not renewing the lease. I'll be out by the end of the week."

"You found another space?" Disbelief tinged his question, not the elation she expected.

"No."

"Then why are you leaving? You were right. I have to honor your lease with Glenn. And you'll be open again in a day or two."

She added the fistful of ladles to the box on her right without a backward glance at him and picked up the roll of packing tape. The squeaky crackle as she yanked the dispenser over the top of the box allowed her a moment to work her response past her tight throat. "It's time to take my sister's advice. I'm moving on."

"Moving on?" Lucas's contemptuous tone set Roma's blood boiling. "You mean running away, don't you?"

She heaved a roll of bubble wrap in his direction. "How dare—"

"No, how dare *you*?" He took another step into the kitchen, his stern glare laughable compared to the seething rage inside her. "I care about you, damn it. And you acted like you cared about me last night. You let me stay. It wasn't just us fucking each other senseless to scratch an itch this time. I gave you part of me when we made love and you let me see your weaknesses."

"*Bastardo*! I'm not weak!" Fury propelled her across the room, fists balled and ready to pound his pronouncements back into him. "I'll show you who's weak, you bastard!"

His hand closed around her wrist as she swung at him. He grabbed the other one a second before her fist connected with his jaw, adding to her anger. Using his greater strength, he lifted her to her tiptoes, bringing her almost eye-to-eye with him. "Do not *ever* use that term around me. Understand?"

A ripple of warning inched along her skin at the controlled wrath in his voice. *Bastard?* Was that the word he meant?

"Do you understand?" He annunciated every syllable, as if she hadn't heard him loud and clear the first time.

"What's the matter?" She raised her eyebrows and met his closed-off stare. "Are you touchy about being called a bastard? Why? Don't you know who your father is?"

He shoved her away as quickly as he'd captured her and bolted outside before she caught her balance. The slam of the door echoed through the chaotic kitchen, confirming she'd hit a highly sensitive nerve. Guilt surged past her anger, and she tried to smother it without success. Had she caught a flash of hurt and humiliation in his eyes?

Then his accusation rushed back to her settling mind. Was she running away or toward something new? Couldn't she do both at the same time?

He cares about me?

Why would he care about me?

He said we made love instead of had sex.

Confusion and regret warred as she wandered toward the worktable full of packing supplies. Longing hit with a vengeance, taking her breath away. She struggled to rebuild the layers of defenses she'd constructed over the last four years, but they weren't strong enough to block the want, the shame, the remorse.

I am weak.

Fighting a wave of lightheadedness that probably signaled the beginnings of another anxiety attack, she locked the back exit and rushed to the walk-in fridge. Cool air seeped into her skin at the entrance, distracting her from the swirling emotions in her head. She couldn't let anyone close enough to make her care again. Getting dumped days before she was supposed to get married would've caused less destruction than witnessing what the man who'd claimed to love her had done to her sister.

Why didn't I see what he was?

She hefted a tub of prepared lemon mix and loaded it onto the cart outside the door, blinking to see through the maddening tears blurring her vision. *Peach. Coconut. Raspberry. Chocolate. Vanilla.*

Leaving the last four flavors for the next trip, she wheeled the load to the sink and dumped the contents of each bucket down the drain. The kaleidoscopic whirls mixed with the running water, diluting the colors and smells into nothing but a nauseating mess.

Like my life?

Lucas had planted the doubts, fed them, and stormed out before they'd bloomed and reseeded. He had no right to tell her she was weak. His reaction to her insult proved he had his own fair share of pieces, some evidently too shattered to fit together anymore.

Glass houses and stones.

Not even attempting to fight the wrath boiling inside him, Lucas heaved a rock into the creek and bellowed loud enough to send a flock of birds scattering from the trees. Why should he care what Roma Denata thought of him? What names she called him?

How can I feel anything for someone so heartless?

Other emotions far outweighed the feelings that had begun to develop overnight, but hurt and anger buried them all. He picked up another rock and hurled it to the far bank. He never should have entertained the idea of staying or having a romantic relationship.

"Lucas?" The apprehension in his mother's voice confirmed what he'd always known. She'd expected him to snap one day, to lose the battle against becoming a monster like his biological father. "Lucas, what's wrong?"

He shook his head and shoved his hands in his pockets instead of picking up a whole handful of stones. "I don't want to talk about it."

A stick cracked behind him and then she laid her hand on his arm. "You've never wanted to talk about it, but I think it's time."

"You don't have to do this." *I can't do this.* "It's best if I leave as soon as the building's ready. You shouldn't have to pretend you're okay with me staying."

She stepped in front of him, the frustration in her expression rivaling his own anger. "Did I ever give you the impression that I regretted getting pregnant with you? You're the one bright spot that came out of a horrific experience and I honestly don't think I'd change what happened if it meant not having you. I survived being violated, but the guilt you carry around breaks my heart. It doesn't matter who your biological father is. He was nothing. The man who raised you as his own child is your dad and he loves you. *We* love you. We want you to stop punishing yourself for something that was never your fault. Only one person did anything wrong, and it wasn't you." She grasped his hands and kissed his cheek. "You remind me that my world didn't end thirty-nine years ago. You and your dad brought me back to life when I thought I wanted to die. Please stay."

Unshed tears burned his eyes and the phantom ache in his chest made speaking impossible.

"I want you to be happy. You deserve to love and be loved." The sadness in her expression was the same agony he'd seen since the day he'd told her about the kid who had said his father was a rapist.

He dropped his gaze from hers, letting his shoulders slump under the weight of thirty years of knowing the truth about himself. "Tell that to the woman who called me a bastard today."

"People say things without thinking, especially when they're in pain themselves. Or they don't realize how much a single word can hurt."

"She knew exactly what she was saying and how much it would cut me. She's about as opposite of her sister as anybody could be."

"Roma and Andria?"

He nodded. "How can they be so different?"

"She went through so much."

"That's why she was my first choice for running the center."

"I meant Roma. Sometimes I think she's suffered more than Andria." His mom grasped his hand and led him along the path that ran parallel to the creek. "She was there."

His stomach dove to the ground. "She saw it happen?"

"Mm-hm. He attacked her when she tried to stop him."

God, that generic "he" who ruins lives. Lucas swallowed against the bile trying to crawl up his insides. "Did he hurt her?"

"Yes, but her injuries weren't life-threatening. A broken arm. A black eye. Some cuts and bruises. And then being arrested for assault with a deadly weapon, when all she did was defend herself."

"Holy hell." The urge to vomit returned with a vengeance, along with the need to pummel the living daylights out of the creep who'd hit her.

"Thankfully, the charges were dropped after Andria corroborated her story, but that was a day or two later, after Roma had already spent at least one night in jail. I wish the Foundation had had the funds to open the center back then. Andria got the help she needed, but I'm not sure Roma ever received counseling or support services for what happened to her. If I'd known the rest of the details back then, I would've found a way to do something for her. When he's someone you know... I can't begin to imagine how all of it affected her." Pausing at the oak that still held remnants of his old tree house, she cast a curious glance at him. "Do you love her? She deserves to be loved as much as you do."

What should've been an automatic no was a silent maybe. He shrugged, still reeling from his mother's revelations about Roma. Her claim about being willing to go to jail for her sister made perfect sense now—because she already had. A second time probably wouldn't make any difference to her.

What about the piece of shit who'd assaulted Andria? Had her rapist been a family member or a close friend? Hindsight always seemed to be twenty-twenty, but Roma couldn't have known what to expect. She'd been a victim too. That would certainly explain her aversion to anything resembling a relationship.

"It's okay if you don't know how you feel. Give it some time. Think about what you really want, deep in your heart." At the crunch of gravel in the distance, she glanced toward the house. "Sounds like your father's home. You're welcome to stay as long as you like, no matter what happens with Roma."

The invitation didn't spark the impulse to run like hell anymore, and her smile matched the one he remembered from his early childhood—before he'd been confronted with the origin of half his DNA. "Thanks, Mom. I love you."

"I love you too, Lucas. Remember, you don't give up on someone you love when they're hurting. *Especially* when they're hurting." She squeezed his hand and then cut across the yard rather than following the path back to the house.

His dad met her partway down the hill, gathering her in his arms and swinging her in a wide circle like he'd been gone weeks or months instead of a few hours. Her joyful laugh carried on the light breeze.

That's what I want. With Roma.

If he stayed, he'd have to let her in and trust that she didn't give a damn about where he came from.

∽

"Lucas?" Andria stood in the open doorway to his office, her bright smile announcing her happiness to the whole damn world. "Do you have a minute? There's someone here to see you."

"Who is it?" The gruffness in his voice didn't seem to bother her, but a full day and then some had passed since he'd walked out on Roma. He also hadn't heard a peep from Ben Kaiser.

"Cliff Darwin. My sister's mechanic."

A guy in a dark-blue jumpsuit stepped around her and wiped his grease-stained hands on the front of his work clothes.

Lucas refocused his attention on the spreadsheet on his computer. "I don't need a mechanic."

"I have some information that might help Roma reopen the gelato shop."

"What kind of information?" Looking up from his laptop, Lucas gestured for his visitor to sit. *This better not be some kind of joke.* "Andria, would you mind closing the door?"

She nodded and shut the mechanic in the room.

Cliff shuffled forward and dropped into the closest chair. "I overheard you and Ben talking at the restaurant the other day, not that I was spying or anything."

"That was a private conversation. If you heard anything, you were listening on purpose. Get to the point."

Picking at his cruddy fingernails, the mechanic grimaced. "I think a girl I picked up at a bar last week got Roma shut down."

Tempering a spark of hope, Lucas closed his computer. "Explain."

"Well, Angelica talked me into taking Barry out for a drive—that's Roma's Barracuda—and Roma was waiting at the garage when we got back. Man, was she ticked off. Anyway, Angelica got mad at me for saying going out with her was a mistake and she didn't like Roma making fun of how young she is. Then she said she was pregnant a couple days ago and threatened to have me arrested if I didn't give her a bunch of money. I asked Roma for advice, even though she got me fired for joyriding in her car, 'cause she's smarter than just about everybody I know." Cliff finally glanced up from his fidgety hands. "Did you know it takes more than a week for a woman to know if she's pregnant?"

Reining in his impatience, Lucas drummed his fingers on the arm of his chair. "Yes. Your point?"

"See, Roma said she was conning me and not to pay her a dime unless a pregnancy test came back positive and she had a paternity test. You know, in case it isn't mine. Angelica about had a fit when I told her what Roma said."

Jesus, you're giving me a headache. "And what does any of this have to do with the gelato shop?"

Cliff scooted forward in his seat. "Oh, Angelica's dad is a health inspector for the county. I guess I forgot to tell you that part."

Why the hell didn't you say that first? Lucas pushed away from the desk and crossed to the coffeemaker, trying to contain his eagerness to fix the most urgent of Roma's problems. "I appreciate you stepping forward with this information, Cliff. In order to help Roma, you need to tell Ben Kaiser exactly what you told me. I'll see if he's available now. And I'm guessing you're here on your lunch hour, so I'll have him pick up something on his way here. Do you want pizza or a hamburger?"

Cliff's eyes widened and he rubbed his stained hands together. "Both?"

CHAPTER 15

With the last box sealed, Roma propped open the service door to prepare for loading. The U-Haul truck blocked the drive behind the building, but not many people were out and about at twelve thirty on a Wednesday night. If they had a complaint, they could take it up with her middle finger.

She wheeled the loaded dolly up the ramp, fighting gravity every inch of the way and hoping this was the heaviest box of the dozens waiting to be moved from the shop to her garage. "I don't care if I have to drag your ass into this truck. You're going in, damn it."

"Need some help?"

Locking her knees with each step, she shoved the load into the empty cavern. Her pulse thumped in her ears as she loosened the straps. "What does a lawyer know about packing a moving truck?"

"That some things are too heavy for one person." Ben Kaiser extended a hand as she tramped down the ramp with the dolly. "You could hurt yourself. You shouldn't be doing this when nobody else is around."

Ignoring his implication that he would handle the wheeled assistant for her, she bumped and rattled back to the kitchen. "I prefer it that way. What are you doing creeping around this time of night?"

He followed her inside. "Late night at the office wrapping up a case, the one I've been trying to reach you about since yesterday, and I saw your lights on. People worry when you don't respond to text messages and voicemails."

"As you can see, I'm fine." Curiosity tried to force her to ask about the case, but she bit her lip and slid another of the heaviest boxes onto the dolly.

"I wanted to update you on the appeal hearing. There isn't going to be one."

A yank on the strap didn't begin to vent her infuriation. "I didn't expect it to happen. Get out of the way or grab a box. And no more talking."

"Don't you want to know why the hearing was canceled?" He crossed his arms and blocked her path to the truck. "Lucas Calloway and I did a little investigating."

"Oh? Did he admit to closing me down?" Scowling to hide any possible sign of interest, she picked up a lighter box and tried to shove past him, but he didn't budge. "Get out of my way, damn it."

"Listen to me, Roma. Lucas had nothing to do with it."

"I suppose you have proof to back that up."

He exhaled, long and slow like he did when Brayden tested his patience. "Your mechanic tipped us off about a young woman who tried to blackmail him. I believe you met her last week when you picked up your car from the garage and then advised Cliff earlier this week when she tried to extort money from him by claiming she was pregnant with his child. She filed the complaint because you thwarted her scheme, and her father was a health inspector for the county—until this morning. The closure has been rescinded."

As much as she wanted to celebrate the vindication, she couldn't change her mind about leaving. Lucas might have cared about her, but calling him a bastard had almost certainly destroyed all his positive feelings for her. Besides, she wasn't capable of love anymore. Even the mere thought of loving a man had chased her from her bed before sunrise when she'd awakened wrapped in his arms. "Thanks, but it's too late. I need to move on."

"What about Andria and your *nonna*? Are you leaving them behind too?"

"What the hell is it with you people, judging me for living my life the way I want to? Andria made her own choice. I didn't ask her to move out. And *Nonna* will support whatever I do." Giving up on trying to squeeze past Ben, she swapped the box for the papers still setting where she'd put them two days ago. "Here, deliver these to your buddy Calloway. He walked out without them the last time I saw him."

"Because you insulted him? Or because you threw him out? I like you, Roma, but you need to learn to get along with people."

"God, not you too." She detoured to her office, willing to wait out his departure. "There's your answer. I'm sick of hearing I have to be nice to everybody. Maybe you do, but I don't. Good-bye, Ben."

His frown disappeared behind her office door as she kicked it shut with her foot.

None of you understand what it's like to know you can never atone for actions that caused irreparable harm. You need to stop thinking you can save me from myself.

Fifteen minutes passed before she chanced another attempt to pack the rental without interference. Thankfully, her lawyer had gone and taken the paperwork with him, letting her work herself to exhaustion in peace.

∽

"Are you okay? I haven't seen or heard from you in two days. Call me, okay?"

"Yes. By my choice. No." Roma deleted her sister's voicemail as she adjusted the towel wrapped around her wet hair.

"Answer your phone please. I'm worried about you."

Delete. Rummaging through the basket of clean laundry, she grabbed a tank, shorts, and underwear. A bra tangled around the tank, but she dropped it on top of the pile in the basket. *Not a chance in hell.*

"Roma, answer your phone. Or at least call me back."

Delete. Every muscle in her body ached like a son of a bitch, but she managed to pull the shirt over her head as the fourth and final voicemail played. Hopefully, the pain relievers she'd taken before she showered would kick in soon.

"Since you won't respond, I'm coming to find you. With Maxine's sixth sense, it shouldn't take long. Oh, and I'm telling *Nonna* about your temper tantrum."

"Damn it. Coffee first." After deleting the last message time-stamped eight minutes ago, Roma settled for underwear and tossed the shorts back in the basket on her way to the kitchen. The scent of strong black Columbian filled the air as she switched from calls to text messages. *"I'm fine."*

Less than five seconds later, her phone vibrated against the counter. *"I'm calling you and you better answer."*

"God, I should've waited until my coffee was done." The slurpy sucking noise of her Keurig almost drowned out the buzzing of her cell. "Hang on a sec, Andria. I'm in the middle of something."

"Make it quick. This is important."

A healthy dribble of milk cooled the brew enough for a sip. Roma followed it up with another and then tapped the speaker icon. "Fair warning. I've had no sleep and I'm on my first cup of coffee this morning."

"You shouldn't have spent the night moving out of the shop. Yes, I heard about your melodramatic run-in with Ben last night, but that's not why I'm calling." A long pause indicated her sister expected her to ask why.

"I'm not in the mood for guessing games, Andria." With her elbows resting on the table, Roma cradled her head in her hands. "If you have something to say, say it."

"What happened between you and Lucas? He won't tell me and you've been missing in action since Tuesday."

Hearing his name made last night's pizza curdle in her stomach. "We had an argument. He called me weak and I called him a bastard. I must've hit a sore spot, because he got mad and left. Good riddance."

"People have feelings, Roma. You can't just go around insulting everybody without some backlash. That word can be incredibly offensive. You need to apologize to him."

"Why should I apologize when—"

"Look, you can either tell him you're sorry or I can tell Nonna what you did."

"You wouldn't."

"Try me. I'm going to text Lucas and ask him to come to your house at noon. That gives you two hours to prepare a suitable apology. And there will be consequences if you aren't sincere. We'll discuss this moving nonsense later."

The line went dead before Roma could refuse. When had her sister become so bossy?

It isn't nonsense and there's nothing to discuss.

Lucas rang the doorbell, caught between craving a glimpse of Roma and hoping her desire to move on had taken her away from the house today. Loving a woman wasn't supposed to be so damn hard, not that he even had a choice in the matter or that she gave a damn how he felt.

The snick of the lock and the inward motion of the six-panel door shifted his roiling stomach into high gear. Then Roma stood framed in the window of the storm door, wearing her usual tank top and shorts. The dark smudges beneath her eyes spoke of little sleep and an adorable pile of messy curls on her head suggested she'd rolled out of bed only a few minutes ago.

I could wake up to that beautiful face every morning for the rest of my life and never get tired of it.

"Come in." Her invitation lacked enthusiasm, but at least she hadn't told him to go the hell away. She shoved on the latch without meeting his gaze.

He swallowed the achy lump in his throat and followed her into the living room. "Andria asked if I could move a potted tree from the sunroom to her office. She said she'd meet me here on her lunch break."

Roma snagged a pillow from the couch as she passed it. Instead of sitting, she hugged the squishy rectangle to her chest and paced to the kitchen doorway. She pivoted toward him, but she stared at a spot near his feet. "She lied."

"Why?" The question snuck out, setting him up for another disappointment.

"She convinced me I should apologize to you." She glanced up and then down again. "I'm sorry for calling you a bastard. It clearly hurt you. And I shouldn't have said those things. It was mean, even for me."

One last shot. I have to take it. He perched on the back of the armchair, a cold sweat crawling between his shoulder blades and up his neck. "I want to tell you why I hate that word."

"You don't have—"

"I want you to know why." Gesturing to the couch, he let out a slow exhale. "You might want to sit for this."

She pursed her lips at him as she crossed the room and plopped into the corner of the sofa closest to him, still clutching the pillow. Her silence warned him she wasn't the least bit comfortable with the idea of talking about his feelings.

He rubbed his damp palms on his shorts, willing his breakfast to stay in his stomach. "I know who my biological father was. His name. What he looked like. He's dead. Since I was about a month old."

"I'm sorry." Her quiet apology was at odds with her typical boisterous and plainspoken demeanor.

"Don't be. He died in prison." Thirty years of knowing what his father was didn't lessen the nausea or the disgust, but he was done with the shame. His eight-year-old self shouldn't have had to live with the knowledge that his existence was based on a single violent act.

"What was he in prison for?" The color had drained from Roma's face, hinting that she didn't really want to know what crime had gotten him incarcerated.

Bracing his elbows on his thighs and clasping his hands, Lucas fought the urge to hightail it out the door and never stop running. He'd done that more times than he could count. *Not anymore.* "He raped my mother."

She gasped and trapped the pillow as she drew her knees to her chest with shaky hands. A tear skittered down her pale cheek, followed by another and another. Her shoulders trembled and a sob broke loose. "I-I...I'm so sorry."

He dropped to his knees in front of her, cradling her face in his palms. "It doesn't define who I am. I'm not him and I have nothing to be ashamed of. The man who raised me as his own son made me who I am. It's taken me a long time to understand and accept that. I'm not just a reminder of that horrific event to my mom, either. She and my dad wanted kids, but he would've supported her no matter what choice she made. I would've too, even though I sometimes wish she'd chosen a different option. I don't know how she's strong enough to look at me and not see the piece of shit who violated her. I still struggle with it."

"It wasn't your fault. You didn't cause it." She squeezed her eyes shut, forcing new streams of tears past her cheekbones. "Not like me."

"What are you talking about? You're not responsible for someone else's violence."

"My...my sister." The gasping sobs started again, and her grief was a palpable, living thing. It lived with her—at home, at work, everywhere she went. "I should've known. Why didn't I see?"

He moved to the couch and lifted her onto his lap, the source of her constant rage finally becoming clearer. "Can you tell me what happened?"

She shook her head and buried her face in his neck.

Armed with one last truth, he kissed the messy knot of curls tickling his chin. "I love you, Roma. I want to help you through this."

Every muscle in her body snapped taut, and she scrambled out of his lap. Backing away from him, she crossed her arms in front of her chest like they could protect her from his declaration. "No, you don't. And I don't need help. There's nothing anyone can do to change what happened."

He swallowed a defensive retort and settled into the cushions. "The past is done. Talk to me so you can let go of the anger. You deserve to be happy."

"How would you know what I deserve? You weren't there." Her voice rose with every syllable, contradicting her claim about not needing someone to lean on.

"I know Andria was raped. It's one of the reasons she was offered the director job at the recovery center. And I also know you saved her. It could've been so much worse if you hadn't shown up. You stopped that monster from—"

"That monster was my fiancé!" She spun away, hiding the anguish on her face but not in her words. "How did I not see what he was? I should've known. It never would've happened if—"

"It never would've happened if he hadn't been a rapist. Period. Placing your trust in someone who should've respected you, your sister, and every other woman wasn't wrong. You couldn't have known. It's his fault. Only his."

"And what about wishing I'd killed him? He's sitting in a mental institution, not even remembering what he did. An inch lower, and that fireplace poker would've ended it."

Following his instincts, he rose from the couch and wrapped his arms around her from behind. "You need to stop blaming yourself."

Although she tensed, she didn't pull away. "But—"

"No buts. You weren't the cause and I'm not the effect. We're two people who suffered collateral damage from events beyond our control. We have to heal, just like my mom and your sister. It's the only way to take away the power their rapists have over us." The jump of her muscles beneath his fingertips made him wish punishing her ex-fiancé for hurting her wouldn't land him in jail. "Will you be my support partner in some private counseling sessions at the center when it opens? I'll be yours if you want me to be."

CHAPTER 16

The gentleness of Lucas's embrace tempted Roma to take him up on his offer, but it required a level of trust she didn't possess. *He was right the other day.* "I'm not strong enough."

His breath caressed her cheek. "I'm not, either. Not by myself. I'm asking you to share the strength you have with me, and I'll gladly share mine with you. I can't do this alone. I don't want to."

"But why me?" She closed her eyes to shut out the dancing colored lights trying to hijack her vision. The beat of his heart pulsed through her shoulder blade, the steady rhythm coaxing her own to slow. *Breathe.*

"Because you understand the guilt better than anyone and it doesn't matter to you whether it's logical or not. It's there. All the time."

He knows.

He covered her hands with his and linked their fingers, creating an interlocked weave. A hoarse whisper tickled her ear. "I need you."

His husky admission touched something inside her, a long-hidden part she'd buried beneath hurt, resentment, and anger. She hadn't allowed herself to need anything or anyone since that fateful day four years ago. If the ice in her heart had held together the shattered fragments of her life, what would happen if it melted?

They're still pieces.

Her equilibrium still not restored, she pulled his arms tighter around her and rested her head against his. "I don't know if anything can fix me."

"You aren't broken, just the expectations you had." He pressed a kiss to her temple and then turned her to face him, compelling her to open her eyes. The detached, always-in-control man he'd been during their business and sexual encounters was gone, revealing the vulnerable side he'd quickly hidden during their last conflict. "I love you, but I don't expect you to take me at my word. I'm asking you to let me prove it. If you decide to trust me, it'll be because I've earned it."

The decision was hers, with no pressure or threat of retaliation, and he'd given her the power to wound him as deeply as she'd been hurt.

His gaze stayed locked on hers. "And no matter what you decide, the storefront is yours. I had my lawyer draw up a contract to transfer ownership to you. I'll help you move back into the shop and cover as many hours as you need until your old employees can come back or you can hire new people. And when I start up the job placement program at the center next month, I'll screen possible candidates if you want me to."

No matter what. No one outside of her family had ever offered her unconditional anything, let alone a building. "You would do that for me? Without expecting something in return?"

He raised her hand to his lips, looking more determined than he'd been about giving her multiple orgasms in his office. "Yes."

Maybe I can do this.

She waited for the lightheadedness and the panic to hit, but the tension in her shoulders eased and her breath came easier. *I can do this.* "You need to do one more thing."

He swept a stray curl from her forehead, inciting a feeling more intense than simple lust. "Name it."

"I swore I would never date again, so you have to move in with me or no deal." The declaration should have sparked a full-blown anxiety attack, but for the first time in four years she was free. Lucas Calloway had promised her the equivalent of the moon, and she wanted to give him the stars.

His tongue slipped out to wet his lips. "Okay. We should seal the deal with a kiss."

"I have a better idea." She walked him backward toward the master bedroom. "If you're going to live here, you need to know where to sleep."

He frowned. "I thought your bedroom was down the hall."

"Not anymore." At the doorway, she yanked her shirt over her head and shoved her shorts and underwear down her legs. "I moved back into this bedroom since you were haunting the room I used while my sister lived here. Take off your clothes."

"I'd rather have you undress me." His salacious grin ignited the same fire that always burned low in her belly when they were in close proximity. "Should I plan on taking the rest of the day off?"

"Yes." Impatient to feel his bare skin against hers, she unbuttoned his shirt and tried unsuccessfully to push it past his shoulders. "Help me."

He cupped her face and touched his lips to her forehead, her nose, and her mouth. "Always."

Captivated by the earnestness in his voice, she stopped struggling with his clothes and took a long moment to savor his kisses. She didn't have to rush to the finish line or close her mind to all but physical sensation. "Show me you love me."

His tongue traced the seam of her lips, asking for instead of demanding entry. She greeted him with a leisurely glide and let his gentle strokes carry her into a slow dance that wooed her heart and soul. Passion flowed from him, but he didn't fight her for control or try to force a reaction from her.

As he nibbled a path to her ear, she grasped his biceps to catch her balance and met with hard muscle and smooth skin. When had he removed his shirt? "I've never been kissed like that before."

"I've never been in love before." He loosened the elastic band from her hair, releasing the messy bun atop her head, and tangled his fingers in the fall of unruly curls. "I've wanted to do this since the first time I saw you."

"Not as much as you wanted to piss me off."

His low, rumbling chuckle vibrated through her body. "I thought it would keep me from wanting more. I was wrong. I love everything about you, including your temper."

"Even when I cussed you out in Italian?"

He scooped her into his arms and carried her to the bed. "Even knowing you were probably telling me to go fuck a yak or threatening to cut off my balls."

"No yaks." She rubbed her cheek along his coarse beard and snickered. "I insulted your dead relatives and said I was going to feed your balls to the pigs. *Nonna* would wash my mouth out with soap if she knew about cursing your ancestors. Even she's used that Roman insult only once that I know of and it was seriously deserved."

"That bad, huh?"

"Oh, yeah. Much worse than feeding the pigs."

"I prefer you didn't do that, either." He laid her on the tangled sheets and stripped off the rest of his clothes while she adjusted the pillow beneath her head. His muscular ass provided the perfect view as he retrieved a condom from his wallet. "Seems like maybe you should say something sexy and romantic to make up for it."

Raising an eyebrow, she took the foil packet and crooked her finger at him. "Let's get you suited up first."

His cock bobbed at her, making her wish he was already inside her. He gasped and groaned as she rolled the latex down his length and then he knelt between her thighs. Feathering his fingertips along her ribs and toward her pussy, he held her gaze. "I'm ready. Are you?"

"*Voglio scoparti finché non ti cade il cazzo.*" She hooked her ankles at his lower back and pulled him closer.

"Mmm. I'll take that as a yes." He inched into her, setting off tremors with every bit of forward progress.

"Kiss me." Grasping the back of his head, she rose to meet him.

The motion drew him deeper into her body, filling her so completely she couldn't imagine ever living without him. Each languid glide of his tongue along hers matched the easy rhythm of his rocking hips, and the warmth of his bare chest bathed her breasts in heat as he tightened his hold on her. They were one body and one heart, an extension of one another in their own private world.

He swelled inside her, amplifying the pleasure that surely surpassed anyone's concept of heaven. An unexpected surge of weightlessness accompanied the onslaught of utter bliss and his cries blended with hers as he joined her.

She wasn't alone and she didn't have to rush away in an effort to ward off a connection. Being connected to him meant being broken didn't matter. He'd given her part of himself and together they could be whole.

His breathing still rough, he collapsed beside her and wrapped his arms around her. "I swear…I can last longer…than two minutes."

Unable to stop a giggle, she nuzzled his fuzzy chin. "You're improving. It was thirty seconds before."

"Ha. Ha. I think your sexy Italian talk might've been too sexy." He smoothed his palm up her spine, setting off a series of aftershocks. "What did you say?"

Another giggle followed a snort. "Are you sure you want to know?"

He shook his head and laughed. "Maybe not, but now you have to tell me."

"Okay, here goes." She tried and failed to keep a straight face. "'I want you so much. Make love to me until your dick falls off.'"

A low, rumbling laugh vibrated through her body again. "Hmm. That sounds like an invitation to stay forever."

His positive spin on her Italian not-quite-sweet nothing sparked a hiccup in her pulse. "It is, *amore mio*."

* * * * *

Want more??? Check out the *Flavor of the Day* bonus epilogue at https://www.mellanieszereto.com/books/book-list-genres-romance-tropes/fotd-bonus-content/!

ABOUT THE AUTHOR

When her fingers aren't attached to her keyboard, Mellanie Szereto enjoys hiking, Pilates, cooking, gardening, and researching for her stories. Many times, the research partners with her other hobbies, taking her from the Hocking Hills region in Ohio to the Colorado Rockies or the Adirondacks of New York. Sometimes, the trip is no farther than her garden for ingredients and her kitchen to test recipes for her latest steamy tale. Mellanie makes her home in rural Indiana with her husband of thirty-three years and their son. She is a 2016 recipient of the RWA Service Award, RWA Chapter Advisor, and a member of Romance Writers of America, Aged to Perfection - Seasoned Romance Writers of America, Contemporary Romance Writers, Fantasy, Futuristic, and Paranormal Romance Writers, Indiana Romance Writers of America, and Northeast Ohio Romance Writers of America.

Email: mellanie@mellanieszereto.com
Website: http://www.mellanieszereto.com
Newsletter: http://eepurl.com/cDEHXL
Facebook: http://www.facebook.com/authormellanieszereto
Amazon: https://www.amazon.com/author/mellanieszereto
BookBub: https://www.bookbub.com/authors/mellanie-szereto
Book+Main Bites: https://bookandmainbites.com/MellanieSzereto
Goodreads: http://www.goodreads.com/mellanie_szereto

If you enjoyed this book, please consider rating or leaving a review on the retailer's website, BookBub, and/or Goodreads. Thanks!

Made in the USA
Lexington, KY
23 November 2019